the

first law

of mo...

D1502019

DATE DUE		
FEB 2 7 2010		
APR 0 7 2010		
JUN 2 2 2012		

11-09

the
first law
of motion

K. R. MOORHEAD

ST. MARTIN'S GRIFFIN ☙ NEW YORK

11-09

14-

This is a work of fiction. All of the characters, organizations, and events portrayed in this novel are either products of the author's imagination or are used fictitiously.

THE FIRST LAW OF MOTION. Copyright © 2009 by K. R. Moorhead. All rights reserved. Printed in the United States of America. For information, address St. Martin's Press, 175 Fifth Avenue, New York, N.Y. 10010.

www.stmartins.com

Library of Congress Cataloging-in-Publication Data

Moorhead, K. R.
  The first law of motion / K. R. Moorhead.—1st ed.
      p. cm.
  ISBN 978-0-312-54729-5
  1. Self-realization in women—Fiction.   2. Psychological fiction.
I. Title.
  PR6113.O65F57   2009
  823'.92—dc22
                                                        2009017047

First Edition: November 2009

10 9 8 7 6 5 4 3 2 1

I have never needed to search for a Muse. The Muse is usually a piece of narcissistic nonsense in female form. Or at least that's what most men's poetry reveals. I would rather a democratic version of the Muse, a comrade, a friend, a travelling companion, shoulder to shoulder, someone to share the cost of this long, painful journey. Thus the Muse functions as collaborator, sometimes as antagonist, the one who is like you, the other over against you.

—*Hallucinating Foucault* by Patricia Duncker

This book was written for
Jason Mark Rodgers.

From one muse to another.

acknowledgments

Thanks to . . . My badass agent, Caroline Hardman at the Marsh Agency; Regina Scarpa at St. Martin's Press; Patricia Dunker for permission to quote from her book *Hallucinating Foucault*; the Get Up Kids for permission to use lyrics from their song "Pabst Blue Ribbon"; all my friends who read drafts, gave honest feedback, and put up with me yammering away about this book all the time, especially Kevin Booth, Greg Shorter, Jen Morley, Alice Pirie, Dan Timms, and James Watson; Andrew Cowan, to whom I owe everything; my grandfather Paul Moorhead, for being someone I always wanted to make proud; my father, Dave Kuhn, for always thinking everything I do is cool and funny; my amazing mother, Mary Moorhead, for encouraging me to do things that are hard, but worth doing; the very talented writer and love of my life, C. D. Rose, for making me want to be a better person. And a special thanks to David. You're a wonderful man.

the
first law
of motion

"WHAT'S WITH THE SCAR?"

He had stumbled toward me from across the party, sloshing cheap, watery beer over the rim of his red plastic cup. I watched it disappear into the ugly carpet.

Now he's standing too close to me, breathing too heavily, and I think about all the undergrads who have puked, pissed, shat, fucked, and spat on that carpet over the years. I drop my cigarette onto it and grind the butt in with the heel of my sneaker.

He presses his giant ham of an index finger into the circular scar on my left upper arm. I want to punch him in the face. When is it OK to touch a complete stranger? CPR, Heimlich maneuver? A life-or-death situation, maybe, and even then I'd be uncomfortable.

I put my hoodie on.

"I was born in Vietnam. It's an inoculation scar." This is bullshit. Actually, it's from when I let some guy I met in a bar burn me with his cigarette just to prove that I could take it.

I can be a real fucking idiot sometimes.

"But you're white."

A genius.

"No shit, asshole." I take a busted pack of Marlboros out of my back pocket and light one.

"Hey, fuck you, bitch." He stumbles back across the room.

Good riddance.

I don't know why I come to these things. House parties attract the world's most boring people. Which most definitely makes me boring. I take a flask out of my hoodie pocket and take a swig. It's not as hard-core as I want it to look because it's whiskey *and* Coke, but I refuse to be seen with one of those plastic keg cups.

Fuck that.

I end up sitting on the back steps leading to the square of cement that somehow manages to pass for a backyard in this godforsaken end of this godforsaken city, rolling a joint. A few randoms stand around smoking cigarettes. A tall guy in baggy corduroys makes his way over to me as I spark up.

Mooch.

"Can I sit down?"

I slide across the step.

"Is that a J?"

"Yeah."

"Can I get a hit?"

Does he know how hard it is to get green in this city right now? I paid good money for this shit.

"Yeah, sure."

He takes a long, no, a fucking luxurious drag on my joint and hands it back. He straightens up, struggling to hold the smoke in his lungs. I take a few light puffs and exhale through my nose. Finally he exhales as well.

"Thanks, I needed that. This party is lame."

"Fair enough."

"Where'd you get that anyway? That's good shit."

"My mom." This is true.

"Ha right. Hey"—he leans in close and hurls his Coors Light breath at me—"you wanna line?"

Fuck yeah.

"Fuck yeah."

A herd of ugly drunk people desperate for a piss shout and bang on the bathroom door. From the sound of it someone's either retching or fucking in there, so I grab him by the sleeve and lead him up to the attic bedroom, which has a latch on it. I don't really know the people who live here, but I've been over a few times with Kat, and once I bought mushrooms from the guy who lives in this room.

I tripped balls that night.

I latch the door and we sit on the bed. The room is cramped with a low, slanted ceiling. He finds an Allman Brothers CD case and cuts up two fat lines with his Delaware County Community College ID before holding the case out to me and handing me a rolled-up five-dollar bill.

Classy.

I blow through what I think is the bigger of the two lines. It's like breathing sand, and it sears down the back of my throat, taking globs of snot with it. I lick the tip of my finger and run it across the CD case. I rub my finger along my gums and they start to go numb almost immediately. I can never remember if that means it's good quality or bad.

Right now I don't care.

I hand him the case back without offering to hold it for him. He balances it precariously on his knee so he can close one nostril and stick the fiver up the other. I will the plastic case to slip. To tip slightly and dump his blow all over this crusty, unmade bed. I can picture him snuffling in the sweaty, stained sheets. Desperate to ingest every last amphetamine particle and anything that happens to come with it. I lean back against the pillows and shut my eyes.

It smells like balls in this room. Every guy's room I've ever been in smells like this.

Testicles.

I hear Backyard Boy blow through his line without incident and put the CD down. The bed shifts and creaks as he moves to lie next to me. I can feel myself coming up. My heart starts beating faster, and my face flushes. He puts his hand on my stomach, under my shirt, and lets it sit there. My stomach tenses.

More anonymous touching.

I don't like it, but I don't move yet. I'm trying to enjoy my come-up. He moves closer to me, and I can feel his thick breath on my ear as he pants and drools like a damned Saint Bernard. He starts slowly rubbing my stomach, and I can feel his dry lips against my neck. He's kissing behind my ear and his hand moves up. Under my bra he's cupping my left tit. Just cupping it, like now that he's got there he doesn't know what to do next. I haven't opened my eyes yet, or moved. As I feel him touching me, each one of my internal organs tightens anxiously as if they may individually throw up at any moment. I imagine my torso filling with organ puke.

He's ruining my high.

I have to get out.

I grab his wrist and remove him from my tit.

"Back off, asshole." I throw my legs over the side of the bed and fix my shirt before standing up.

"What the hell's the matter?"

"I don't fuck cokeheads." I light a cigarette and walk out.

"Hey, fuck you, bitch!"

As I jog down the stairs I wonder who else I can piss off tonight. Maybe score the "Hey, fuck you, bitch!" hat trick. Pathetically, I'm afraid he'll come running down after me in the midst of some coke rage, drag me back upstairs by my hair, and rape me in that cramped, testicle-scented bedroom. My stomach heaves, and I taste acid on the back of my tongue. I swig out of my flask. Almost empty.

Time to go.

Out on the street I manage to regain some of my high. It's September but it's still warm, and I leave my hoodie unzipped. I check my watch: 3:30 A.M. Maybe I'll get a train to New York and see Jason. I'm pretty sure they run this late. I find my phone and call him.

"Well, hello lady," Jay answers.

"Yo Jay, what's up?"

"Nothing, just heading to the Phoenix for last call. What're you doing?"

"Nothing. I was at a house party, but it sucked so I bailed. Some guy gave me a fat line though, and now I'm all jacked up with nowhere to go."

"Come up. I have to work this weekend, but we can definitely hang out."

Shit. Work. I forgot all about that.

"Fuck, I'm meant to be at the café tomorrow at, like, nine."

"Call out."

The thought of forcing myself to smile through a six-hour shift without throwing scalding coffee on some helmet-haired real-estate bitch seems downright impossible.

"Yeah. Sounds good. I'll be at your apartment in, like, three hours."

"Awesome."

I decide to walk to the train station since I'm already in West Philly. About two blocks in, the fear hits me. I'm in West Philly at almost 4 A.M. on a Friday night. The chances of me getting raped, mugged, and murdered are, like, one in one.

No, fuck that. I hands down refuse to be afraid. Besides, I have no cash on me for a cab.

Chestnut Street's practically deserted save for a few taxis, their yellow paint looking flu-sick under green traffic lights. I pass a pile of newspapers, rising and falling almost imperceptibly with the labored sleep breaths of someone underneath. I kick an empty Burger King cup ahead of me and jog to catch up with it. I consider kicking it again but just stamp on it instead, relishing the crunch of plastic-coated cardboard.

As I cross Thirty-ninth Street, I see two young black men walking toward me. My heart starts racing, and I can feel the anxious little knots starting. That's it. This is it. I'm fucked. As they get closer I contemplate crossing the street but am so afraid of them at this point that the idea of doing something so stereotypically offensive seems like a death wish. We are at opposite ends of the same block, and I can hear my blood thundering in my ears. As I approach them, they are talking in low voices, but they go silent when they see me.

"Yo, shorty." The taller of the two smiles at me and sucks his teeth. I smile back but don't make eye contact. "Where you going?" He flicks his head at me as I walk past him. Slick, bald head. Wide, sly smile. He's gorgeous.

Why don't I ever date black men? I don't even ever fuck them. Most likely I'm racist. We all are.

"Home." I can feel his eyes burning into me as I pass him.

"Can I come?" he asks my back.

"Nah, sorry." I throw back over my shoulder.

"Aw, too bad, girl."

I look back as they turn to walk away, and blush.

The expansive, domed ceiling of Thirtieth Street Station spreads above me. A few people list about on the long wooden benches set one in front of the other. I've never noticed how similar to a church it is. And how in a train station, just like in a church, there's no difference between a passenger and a bum at this time of night.

I stare at the big schedule board as it spins and clacks updates at me and will my brain to process stimuli. It is now 3:47 and the next train to Trenton is departing at 3:49. I dig blindly in my bag for my wallet and buy a ticket from the credit card machine along with one from Trenton to New York. I run to Platform 13 West, take the steps down two at a time, and slide onto the train seconds before the doors shut. The car is almost empty so I stretch out on a three-seater. My head is swimming. Picking up a discarded *Philadelphia Weekly*, I try to read but can't focus.

I certainly can't sleep.

I entertain myself by picking filth from under my nails with a safety pin. How do my fingernails get so dirty? I'm not a mechanic for Christ's sake.

No one has come around to collect tickets by the time we pull into Trenton station an hour and a half later.

Standing on the platform waiting for the NJ Transit train to New York, I wonder if people can tell I'm on coke. Shit, I don't even like coke. It just makes me nervous. More nervous. I try to avoid sniffing or touching my nose at all, but that just makes me want to do it more.

Whatever. I'm not even *on* coke. What's one line?

There's hardly anyone on the platform. I light a ciga-rette, and an old lady sitting on a bench in the middle of the platform peers over her thick plastic frames at me.

"You can't smoke that down here." She gestures to-ward a plastic No Smoking sign that someone has clev-erly drawn a cock on in permanent marker. There are a few sparse hairs on the balls and some crude droplets spurting from the tip.

I nod at her and walk toward the other end of the platform, taking my cigarette with me. Fuck that, Wrin-kles, there's no one down here. Besides, underground is the same as outside. And what the fuck are you doing waiting for a train at four in the morning?

At the other end of the platform a young guy leans against a pillar. Probably a student. He has iPod head-phones in his ears and taps his foot lightly. I can't help but wonder what he's listening to. He's not unattract-ive, but by no means hot.

He looks a little like Daniel. Same thick blond hair and sandy five o'clock shadow. My stomach lurches at a flash of memory. The last time we talked.

He hadn't spoken to me in months and then I got a phone call. Out of the blue. "Have dinner with me." I owed him that much. We went to Rembrandt's, got drunk, laughed like we used to. We ended up at his apartment, got stoned, talked like we used to. He kissed my arm. I stopped him. His eyes swelled with drunken, angry tears. "I can't do this. I can't be friends with you.

It hurts too much. You have to understand that this is harder for me than it is for you." I walked out and haven't seen him since.

I did understand.

I do understand. Present tense.

I swallow the memory as Daniel's pale imitation catches my eye, and I smile crookedly before dragging on my cigarette. I extend the pack toward him. He looks at me, takes one, and removes the headphones as I light it for him. I want to go home with him tonight. A zipless fuck, my mom would have called it.

"Thanks."

"Sure. What're you listening to?" I hope it's not something lame and yet assume that it is.

"Arcade Fire."

I've heard of them, but I don't know shit about them or any of their music.

"Oh, awesome. They're really good."

"You going to the show this weekend?"

"Oh no, couldn't afford it." Let me guess. "It's at Irving Plaza, right?"

"Yeah." Predictable. "That's why I'm staying in the city this weekend. I go to school in Jersey."

Also predictable.

"Oh cool. Why so late?"

"What?"

"Why are you going to the city so late tonight?"

"Oh. I bartend and didn't get off work till two."

"Fair enough."

"What about you? Why are you going to the city so late?"

All coked up and nothing to do. "Meeting a friend. Last minute."

"I'm staying with a friend in Brooklyn."

"East Village." I point at myself. I am suddenly aware of how lame I must seem.

"Cool. Well, he's having a party after the show tomorrow night. It's right off Bedford at South Fourth. Apartment 7J. Bring your friend." He thinks my friend is another girl.

"Yeah, definitely." I don't know what else to say. He puts his headphones back in, and we stand in silence until the train comes.

Whatever.

On the train he sits a few seats behind me. I take a sneaky glance back to see what he's reading. *Naked Lunch*. He might be a lost cause.

In the sharp-cornered, store-lined passages underneath New York Penn Station I catch a glimpse of him heading toward the A/C/E downtown. Ending up sitting in a subway car with him at this point would just be painfully awkward, so I slip into a coffee shop. I buy a small coffee that I don't really want and load it up with sugars and creamer. Taking my time, I walk with my coffee through the station, following the blue signs for the A/C/E past darkened storefronts latticed with metal grating. When I get to the turnstiles there's no one there so I hop it. Fuck. I'm probably on camera. I hope the train comes before any transit police. I don't even respect real cops.

I dash down the long corridor leading deeper into the New York underground and onto the platform. It's deserted, and no sign of a train. I walk casually to the far end of the platform and sit on a grimy metal bench. I put my head in my hands. My face is sticky with sweat and the very specific grime that accumulates in the air of underground train and subway stations. It smells like piss.

How very predictable.

I get off at Fourteenth Street, where a few living, waking humans are actually walking around. Cleaning women in sensible shoes heading to work, subway drivers who are just coming off the night shift. Their heavy black boots scraping against cement as they shuffle up and out of the underground. A stooped, grayed black man slumps against a pillar on the platform, playing the flute. The tune is familiar.

"Honky Tonk Women."

It occurs to me that he starts work earlier than I do so I give him a buck. Then it occurs to me that I still have to call the café and tell Rachel McBitchface that I'm not coming in *again*. I can't face it.

I'm not even aboveground yet.

•　　•　　•

I follow gray signs for the L train heading toward Brooklyn. There's a train on each track, waiting. This is the end of the line, and the trains sit here for millions of years before heading back across Manhattan. The sign that should tell me which train will be leaving next is busted, so I have to guess. I head toward the train on my right. Just as I do, the train on my left clicks into action and begins whirring. The doors start to close.

Fuck.

I go for it.

The doors close on my pathetically outstretched arm, and it is actually surprisingly painful. I wedge my fingers in the doors and wrench them open. Gasping, I stagger into the subway car. There aren't many people in the car, but those who are obviously aren't happy about being anywhere this early in the morning. I'm sure they can tell that I haven't been home all night and will probably sleep through the entirety of their hideously boring day.

And I'll sleep like a baby.

I sit on the smooth plastic seats of the newly redesigned L train and take a deep breath. I'm sweating at my hairline and under my arms. I take off my hoodie and tie it around my waist. This makes me look like a giant loser, but for right now I couldn't give a shit. I nod off and wake up at Third Avenue.

I know I know the code to get into Jason's apartment, but I can't for the life of me remember what it is. I call him.

"Jay, what's the code for your front door?"

"Eight-nine-seven-six but I'm upstairs, I'll just buzz you in."

"Cool."

As I enter Jason's tiny second-floor apartment on Avenue B I can see him at the end of the short, narrow hallway. Sitting in his miniscule kitchen/living room, he takes a massive hit off a massive bong. He looks up as I come in, expertly holding smoke in his lungs.

"Brunch?" he asks in a constrained voice before exhaling.

"Definitely. I don't have much of an appetite, to be honest." I sit on the love seat that touches wall on both sides.

"Hit this." He hands me the bong. My lungs strain from chain-smoking Marlboro Reds all night, and I don't get a very good hit. "Do it again." On the second hit I allow the smoke to push against the inside of my chest cavity, expanding my ribs. I suck it all in slowly and choke back my urge to cough. I let it sit there, seeping through all the tiny tubes and irritated tissue, making me feel heavy. I exhale.

"That's my girl. Now do whatever you need to do,

wash your face, brush your teeth. You look like you got in a fight."

"I fought the night, and I won, motherfucker."

"Fuck yeah."

We manage to get outdoor seating at Mogador because it's only eight thirty. In two hours this tiny basement café will be packed with "brunchers" sitting around tiny tiled tables in fashionable shoes, designed by Italians I've never heard of, and planning their day of shopping in Soho stores I'm glad I can't afford.

I don't get it.

Jay and I sit under the awning out front in giant matching sunglasses. Jason's are black, mine tortoise. We're both wearing black hoodies, jeans, and Chuck Taylors. We didn't plan it—that's just the uniform. We wear the same thing every day. Like cartoon characters. We look like everyone and no one.

We both go to light our cigarettes at the same time and just light each other's instead.

When the waitress comes Jason orders for both of us, poached eggs, smoked salmon, English muffin, latte. How *so very* New York.

"So how have you been?" Jay stirs sugar into his latte.

"Generally a miserable bitch, as per usual."

"You were doing better when I saw you last month."

"That's because I was getting laid last month. I'm not getting laid this month. Apparently, I've fucked everyone in Philly. I swear that place is just a small town posing as a big city. I can't step out my fucking door without running into a drunken mistake or a boss who's fired me."

"Fair enough, but you could get laid if you wanted to. Besides, you're unhappy either way." He's got a point there. "Are you taking those new meds they gave you?"

"No." It kills my sex drive. Among other things.

"Good. It'll kill your sex drive. And the last thing you need is to not even be able to give yourself an orgasm."

"Hallelujah, Brother."

"So did your boss have puppies when you called out today?"

Oh shit.

"Oh shit."

"You forgot."

"I'm fucked up. What time is it?"

"Eight forty-two."

"Shit, I'm supposed to be there in, like, fifteen minutes."

I step away from our table with a finger in one ear as the phone rings.

"Tuscany Café."

"Hello, Rachel?"

Shit. Play it cool.

"Yes?"

"It's your favorite employee."

"What is it?" She doesn't sound happy to hear from me.

"Well, I know I'm supposed to be there in, like, fifteen minutes, but I literally just tripped down my front stairs on the way out, and I think I really fucked up my ankle." I could've done better than that. My brain's fried.

"No, don't do this to me again. Are you bailing on me for your shift today?"

She's not buying it.

"Well, the thing is, I thought it'd be fine, but it's really swelling up and gone all black-and-blue. I can't really walk on it." Can't back down now.

"This is, like, the third time this month. You are really screwing me over."

"I'm really sorry, Rach. I don't know what to do. Kat wants to take me to the emergency room."

"Look. Don't come in today. Go to the emergency room. But don't bother coming in after today either. I don't need this shit."

Busted.

"I just got fired." I put my phone on the table.

"You fucked up your ankle? What a crap lie. You sucked at that." He's right.

"Shut up. I've been awake for, like, thirty-six hours."

"I could have come up with something twice as good on half as much sleep."

"That's probably true. Fuck it, I hated that place anyway. At least I'll always have the bar job. That place is such a joke I could burn it down and they still wouldn't sack me."

"Will you make rent?"

"For October, yeah. After that, we'll see."

"I don't know why you don't just move up here. You know I could get you a job and an apartment. I know everyone." This is true.

"You know I don't want to live in New York." I tried it once. For a year, and it just didn't fly. It's a very specific kind of person that can make a life in New York. Jason is it. He wants to know everyone, be everywhere. He cares about what's new, where things are going.

I don't.

"Well, where the hell do you want to live then?"

"I don't know. Anywhere. Somewhere in southern Europe. In a villa with my beautiful Italian artist husband. With babies and border collies running around everywhere."

"Ha. That's the title of your autobiography."

"What is?"

"Babies and Border Collies."

We wander down St. Mark's looking for fingerless gloves. Stalls lining the street sell cheap sunglasses, hats, and jewelry. T-shirts reading "Fuck Dick and Bush," "I do what the voices in my head tell me to do" and "100% Bitch" hang in shop windows.

"I have to work at the restaurant tonight," Jason tells me as he takes a drag off my cigarette.

"That's cool. I'll try and get some sleep. There's a party in Brooklyn we could go to." Was Train Station Boy hitting on me? I must've looked like shit.

"You hate house parties. And who do you know in Brooklyn?"

"Just some guy I met at the train station."

"I get it, you little minx."

"He's not that hot."

"What's his name? Maybe I know him."

"Doubt it. He goes to school in Jersey."

"Jersey? I thought you knew better."

"I don't want to marry him, I just want to fuck him."

"Fair enough."

I fall asleep on the love seat in Jason's apartment and I wake up around six as Jay's getting ready for work. My ears are ringing. Where is that bong?

"Jay, where's the bong?"

"On the TV." He's shaving. His reflection in the bathroom mirror faces me. I carefully stand up, carefully grasp the bong, and carefully sit down again.

"I feel like asshole."

"Come in if you get hungry. We'll feed ya."

I find a lighter and hit the bong. Exhaling, I lie back. The remote is digging into my thigh. I turn the TV on. *My Super Sweet 16* is on MTV. Glossy girls, pink with puberty, giggle and bounce across the screen. Strutting and preening. Pouting and pursing in vapid succession. Stupid fucks. I remember caring about things when I was sixteen. Not saying the Pledge of Allegience, free condoms in high schools, who our next president would be. Not cars and clothes and money. Now I know that it doesn't matter what I care about. So I don't bother caring anymore.

Maybe these girls have the right idea.

I turn the sound off and eventually fall asleep again.

When I wake up it's dark. My head feels better. The brash white glare of the TV inside the apartment competes with the pink fuzzy streetlight of a Saturday night in the East Village as it seeps through the kitchen window. The TV is quiet, but grinding guitar chords float in from the bar below. What time is it? I find my phone. 10:43. Shit. I slept for ages. Jay gets off at twelve, maybe one. Plenty of time to get a few free mojitos in. I rip a few heavy bong hits and get in the shower. It feels perfect. I forgot how incredible a stoned shower could be. I wish I had a cold beer in here as well. I didn't pack anything so I don't have any clean underwear. Guess I'm going commando tonight. I put on one of Jason's thrift store T-shirts. It says "Upper Darby Youth Soccer" on it. It's a little big, but it makes my boobs look good. The Indian summer is in full swing so I decide to walk to Soho.

Out on the street nouveau-punk rockers spill out of a nameless bar and litter the sidewalk. Orange hair, red plaid, black leather, silver metal, they glitter like marbles left on schoolyard blacktop. To skirt them I have to step into the street so I cross it. I light a cigarette. New York's only fun when the weather's nice.

Why do I want to go to this party so badly? Just for the chance to make out with someone who looks a little like my ex and blatantly isn't anything like him? I'd be disappointed if he was. But probably more so if he wasn't.

Even though he isn't speaking to me, Daniel still speaks to Mom. His parents aren't exactly aloof but definitely removed. They're the kind of people who would treat their kids like kids for as long as they live. Mom isn't like that, so Daniel connected with her right away. She treated him like an adult, so he came to her with problems he'd never go to his own parents with. Mom gives excellent advice. And once we split, I couldn't begrudge him so helpful a relationship. But through her, I did try to keep tabs on him. He wasn't doing well. He hated his job and law school and hadn't seen anyone since me. He never even wanted to go to law school. Never talked about it in the two and some years we were together. Then suddenly, he's talking about needing some sort of direction in his life. He was an artist, a writer, a wanderer at heart. But something—pressure from his parents, fear of growing up, I'll never really know—made him feel as though his life didn't matter unless it was lucrative. And law school seemed the obvious idea. It gave me the ability to later justify my breaking up with him by saying we "wanted different things out of life," "we had different goals," "our lives were going in different directions." But really, when I did it . . . it was because I was bored. Bored with school, with sex, with my entire life. I just needed something to change.

He became dispensable.

By the time I get to Houston it's 11:30. Houston Street is wide the way a river's wide. The thought of crossing it can be daunting. I don't jaywalk Houston. I wait for the sign. I go when I'm told. I'm pretty baked and therefore manage to get myself lost in Soho. I wander for a while, looking for familiar landmarks and finally find myself on the corner of Thompson and Spring. I ask what looks like an NYU grad student which way Prince is, and head where he points.

Cubana Café is halfway down the block. It's a basement café with a blue and white awning. It seats about eight comfortably, but somehow they manage to squeeze in seating for forty. No one in the restaurant is Cuban. The food is all made by Mexicans and it's fucking delicious.

I descend the stairs and walk in the open door. Jay is behind the tiny corner bar, polishing its tiny colored tiles. I sit in front of him.

"Feeling better?"

"Much. I need a drink, *por favor*." I say it like a midwestern housewife, pore fayver.

"Done and done." He crushes ice, lime, mint leaves, and sugar by hand before shaking it all up with Cuban rum and soda and pouring it out for me.

"Mmm. Grassy-ass. May goosta."

In the next forty-five minutes I down four more of those and am three sheets to the wind, well on my way to six.

Jason's been throwing back the Jamesons like someone's paying him to do it and isn't particularly steady on his feet either. He brings me a bowl of chicken and vegetable soup as he's cleaning up. It's made of real food. Fresh things. Things that crunch.

As we stumble up to the street, I light a cigarette.

"Finally. I hate this smoking ban, man. It's a pain in the ass."

"At least it's nice out."

"Yeah, don't expect me to come visit you this winter. Fuck that. Philly may be boring, but at least I can smoke inside."

"You'll come up. You'd go insane down there all winter."

"At least they have that lovely mental hospital. I'll be fed, watered, and heavily sedated."

"Well, you could certainly use a vacation."

We take the train out to Brooklyn. People in our car glare at us because we're talking really loudly. We don't give a fuck. Off the train we head toward a squat apartment building on the end of a row of warehouses. All the buildings here are or were warehouses. Square and flat with massive black windows, gaping like eyeless sockets.

"I have a feeling this is going to be a total sausage party. You might even bag yourself a straight." I nudge Jason.

"I like my men like I like my coffee . . ."

"Homophobic?"

The apartment is one huge studio with floor-to-ceiling windows that's been partitioned off into bedrooms with cheap drywall. It looks as though, if you leaned too heavily, you could take the whole place down. I scan the crowd for Train Station Boy and find him in a far corner, chatting with a short blond guy. He's blatantly flirting.

Shit. Fag alert.

I introduce him to Jason.

"Hey man, I'm Jason." They shake hands.

"Sean."

I leave them to it.

He wasn't hitting on me; I'm just such a fag hag that other gay men can smell it on me a mile away.

That's depressing.

I peer in the fridge. It's fairly well stocked with cans of Red Stripe. I put two in my bag, one in each pocket of my hoodie and crack open a fifth. There's a door in the kitchen leading onto a *West Side Story* fire escape. Ex–art school kids are staggered up and down the fire escape stairs in twos and threes. At the top, a skinny guy leans against the railing, smoking. A mass of silky, black curls surrounds his head. Black horn-rims perch on his beak of a nose. He's probably Jewish, grew up in Long Island. He's actually pretty hot. Lean, sharp features. That unmarred, olive oil skin. Too skinny but taller than me at least. He's wearing a tight red T-shirt with the white outline of a robot on it. His ribs show through it.

I bet he's a graphic design major; he made the shirt in his screen-printing class. I ask him for a light even though there's a lighter in my back pocket.

"Sure." He whips out a Zippo with a skull and cross-bones on it.

Hipster.

Humans are suckers for a talisman.

After about twenty minutes, I've killed three of my beers and given him two. I really have to pee. I mean I *really* have to pee. He's been yammering on for the past ten minutes about musical genres I didn't even know existed. I've been saying things like, "Yeah, definitely," and, "No, totally."

"But what I'm mainly into right now is, like, electro-nu-wave girl bands. But, like, the dancier stuff."

My bladder is about to burst.

"Yeah, definitely. Look, I'm sorry, but I really hafta pee. Don't go anywhere." Shit, I hope I don't lose him.

"Yeah, cool."

I dash inside. As is the rule with house parties, there's some sort of satanic ritual sacrifice, or some shit, going on in the bathroom, and no one can even begin to hope to actually use it for a fucking piss. I walk out the front door into the hallway. Shitshitshitshitshit. I am going to pee my pants. And if I don't get back soon Sexy McSkinnyface might wander off and start sniffing the ass of one of those short, spiky girls. He's pretty boring but I've put in too much time at this point to let that happen. I jog down to the end of the hall, holding my crotch. There's a door leading to a cement stairwell. I run down two flights, scrabbling with my belt buckle, before squatting in a corner. The piss hits the cement and splashes back on my ass. Fuck, I'm practically pissing on my own shoes. I wiggle my ass in a vain attempt to dry off, then pull my jeans back up, checking for wet spots.

Back in the party I make my way to the fire escape. No shit. He's still there. I grab some more beers from the fridge and head outside.

"Hey." I hand him a beer.

"Thanks. I was hoping you'd come back. I've gotta couple of Es. You want one?"

What is it with people just giving me drugs? Do I look like that much of a burnout? Is this my life?

"Yeah, definitely."

He digs in his shoulder bag for a bit before producing two tablets. They look like thick aspirin. I inspect mine, as if I can actually tell anything by looking at it. I'm taking an unidentified pill given to me by a complete stranger. Smart. Well, at least he's taking one too, and besides, Jay is here. Somewhere.

"Bottoms up." I take the pill with a swig of beer. He does the same.

•   •   •

Forty-five minutes later I still don't feel anything, and Fire Escape Boy hasn't made a move. We've left the fire escape and wandered into one of the bedrooms where a few people are listening to *Transformer* on an old record player and smoking a bowl. We are sitting on the bed, out of the smoking circle, drinking beers and talking about more bands I've never heard of when Jay sticks his head in the door.

"There you are. I've been looking all over for you. Oh hey, Jesse. I didn't know you were here." Jay and Fire Escape Boy shake hands. "How's it going, man?" Of course Jason knows him.

"Not bad."

"I see you've met my friend, Thelma. She's visiting from Philly this weekend." Thelma. What an asshole. Although it suddenly occurs to me that after all this time we have yet to exchange names.

"Oh yeah. I've been telling her about Clap Your Hands Say Yeah's new album. Have you heard it yet?"

"Uh, no. Not yet." Jay looks down at me. I shrug. "Has she been telling you about how she spent this summer with the Sea Turtle Protection Society in Greece?" I'm not in the fucking mood for this, but the rules stipulate that I must play along. Last time I was in New York he told some girl that I had just been in Tokyo doing my Ph.D. in contemporary Japanese art. I spent the next twenty minutes making up

Japanese-sounding names for the video and performance artists I'd supposedly been studying.

"You didn't tell me you were in Greece."

"Oh yeah, for about six weeks."

"What were you doing?"

"It was volunteer work. We slept in tents near the beach, and every morning we had to survey for new turtle nests." What the fuck am I talking about? "At night we walked the shoreline, hoping to catch the mother turtles actually laying. Then we tagged them." Jason's better at this game than I am, but I do okay. As my lie evolves, I can feel myself coming up. My body warms. My heart beats faster. But it's different from the coke, more gentle. Suddenly, everything feels . . . comfortable. Chemically engineered contentment. I didn't even remember what "good" felt like until just now.

I feel good.

"Wow, that must have been really interesting."

"Hmm?" What the hell are we talking about? Right. Turtles. "Oh yeah. It was . . . interesting. . . . Can I have another pill?"

Me and Fire Escape Boy each take a second pill, and he gives Jason one as well. Jason pulls me out into the living room.

"Excuse us for a second."

Fire Escape Boy nods.

"What?"

"Are you going home with Jesse tonight?"

"Who?"

He jabs a thumb toward the bedroom door.

"Oh right, Fire Escape Boy. Yeah, hopefully."

"OK, good. I'm gonna take Sean back to Ave. B."

"Who?"

"I'm guessing he's Train Station Boy to you."

"Oh right."

"If you get stuck, call me. I'll leave my phone on."

"Cool. Good luck."

"Thanks. Do you think he's hot?"

"Who?"

"Sean, asshole."

"Yeah, definitely."

"All right, I'll see you tomorrow." He kisses me on the cheek. "Be safe."

"You too."

I go back in the bedroom. I feel amazing, beautiful, confident, and all those other meaningless advertisement words that come to mind when I'm pilled to the gills. I feel like a shampoo ad.

"So are you taking me home or what?"

"Uh, yeah. Definitely."

On the way out Fire Escape Boy and I make out in the hallway, the stairwell, outside against the building, and every few blocks or so until we reach his apartment. Kissing feels amazing. Bricks dig into my back and it feels amazing. I can feel everything at once. I look past him. His hair is so soft. His tongue is in my mouth. Warm hand against my back. We're walking and I step in gum. I can feel it suck at the cement as I lift my foot. It feels amazing.

His apartment is not unlike the one we just left, a partitioned studio. The bed in his room is lofted, only a few feet from the ceiling. Underneath is a cluttered desk, across the room, a chest of drawers. And as expected, it smells like balls. We climb the ladder to his bed, which he can barely sit up in. The wall in front of me is littered with movie posters.

Bad movie posters. Not bad movies, just . . . clichéd. *A Clockwork Orange, Trainspotting, Scarface.* The old standbys. Fuck, maybe he's a film student. Did he tell me his major?

Whatever. I'm sure I didn't ask.

What the fuck's his name again?

He offers me another pill. I'm already so high. I'm soaring. So I accept it.

To my left I can't see floor, only window, and beyond that, the city, glittering like broken glass. I feel like I'm hovering above it.

Kissing, we lie back on the bed. Everything around me is soft. He's above me, his hair grazing my forehead. Taking his glasses off, he reaches behind me and places them on the pillows. He smells like boy. With my nose in his chest I slide my hands under his shirt, feeling each of his ribs through his smooth skin. I press my palms against him, trying to absorb the warmth through my pores.

This feels good. And that's "feel" in the tactile sense of the word.

And that's because of the drugs.

I'm suddenly very aware that I'm on drugs. That I only feel this good because I'm on drugs.

Drugsdrugsdrugsdrugsdrugs.

He sits up to take off his T-shirt, bending not to hit his head. I focus on his solar plexus. I don't look at his face. He kisses me. I'm aware of my teeth, of his tongue on them.

I try to ignore my teeth, my fingertips, my inner thighs. I try to ignore the fact that I know I'm on drugs and just enjoy the way they're making me feel. But I'm conscious of every little movement . . . that every little part of me . . . is making at every fucking moment.

Fuck off, teeth.

I try not to remember how boring I think he is, but trying not to remember is really just the same thing as remembering.

It shouldn't matter right now. But it nags me.

Boringboringboringboringboring.

Fuck off, brain, and just let me enjoy this.

Something.

For once.

We slowly, deliberately undress each other, careful

not to get tangled. He doesn't seem to notice that I'm not wearing underwear. Naked, he lies on top of me and I can feel his hard-on.

By the time he gets the condom on and climbs back on top of me, I'm over it. Or outside of it, really. My all-encompassing consciousness of the entirety of this situation has officially ruined it for me. You got me, brain. Good one.

I'm still going to go through with it. Because I've never been very good at calling it off once I've gone this far, no matter how often I've wanted to. Hopefully, my skin will enjoy it, thanks to the E, but now I can't. Shit, I can't even experience it.

I can only watch.

It's a movie. Whoever has been cast as me is slimmer, hair shinier. Her body moves as a body should move in a tasteful sex scene, one that is not gratuitous, but necessary to the plot. She makes the right noises.

Does he think I'm enjoying this? Shouldn't I be? Is he?

I watch him lick my nipples, feebly finger what is becoming my quite dry vagina, and eventually start to fuck me. Thank god for lubricated condoms. I writhe and moan like an amateur porn star but really, where I am, on the other side of my imaginary lens, I can't feel it. It's not me.

Suddenly, the film burns up in the projector. The scene is over practically before it started.

He's done.

Thank god.

I'm still up and the bed feels amazing . . . or some other word that's better than amazing that I'll come up with tomorrow when I'm not up to my tits in Ecstasy . . . but I'm speedy and the thought of spending the morning with this guy asking me to touch his face is appalling. I'll leave, head back to Jay's.

"I'm gonna go." I rummage in the twisted sheets. It smells like latex and vagina. I'd be embarrassed if I actually knew this guy.

"Wait, you don't have to go. I'm still up."

Does he mean from the pills or his dick?

"Where the hell is my underwear?" I ask myself, before remembering that I wasn't wearing any.

"You don't have to leave right now."

Yes I do. "Yeah, I'm gonna go." My jeans are crumpled on the corner of the bed, behind him. I reach around him and grab them. I avoid touching him. Skin-to-skin contact. How the fuck am I gonna get dressed up here? How the fuck did I get *undressed* up here? I throw my jeans off the bed. I can't find my bra. Fuck it. He can have it. A souvenir. I throw my shirt over the side and climb down the ladder naked. This can't be a pretty picture.

"Can I call you?"

My knee smacks the corner of his desk as I stumble and hop into my jeans.

"Fuck." Through clenched teeth. But it doesn't really hurt. Shit, even pain feels good on Ecstasy.

"You alright?"

"Fine." As I put my T-shirt on.

"So, can I call you?"

Fuck no.

"What?" In one movement I grab my bag and slide into my sneakers. I'm out the door.

"Can I call you?" he shouts after me.

"Uh, sure." I call over my shoulder. I'm in the living room, hand on the front door knob.

He calls from the bedroom, "But I don't even have your number!"

I'm out the door, in the hall, downstairs, and back on the street. My heart slams in my ears.

Well, that was pointless.

It's gotta be close to five. The dawn air is warming up and feels silky against my skin. The sky is slowly brightening, but I can't tell where the sun is. It's going to be a hazy day. It'll probably rain.

I have no idea where I am and spend at least an hour wandering through Brooklyn. It's ugly here. Finally I find a bodega that's just opening. The man at the counter directs me to the train in broken English. I buy a cup of coffee and a fresh pack of cigarettes. My hands are trembling as I take my change. Both the coffee and the smoke taste amazing and feel slick and watery, like mercury sliding down my throat.

After a few wrong turns, I find the train and slide into the corner of a seat. Shielding my eyes from the harsh lighting.

When did sex become this? This pointless, completely unenjoyable act that I feel so detached from?

And why do I keep doing it anyway?

Maybe it's because I remember when it was good. Maybe because there was a time when fucking somebody meant something. When fucking Daniel meant something. Before it was "fucking." But then I left him and started fucking anything that winked.

Not long after we broke up, when we were trying to be friends, we went to the Bards one night with his friends Mike and Tim. Tim fucking O'Toole. Talk about an appropriate name.

We got drunk. Tim threw tequila down my throat all night, and somewhere in the evening Daniel wandered home. I didn't even know he had left. I tumbled blindly into a cab with Tim and ended up at the ass end of the city in his massive exposed-brick apartment having some of the worst drunken sex of my life. I spent the whole time trying to convince myself I was enjoying some aspect of the encounter, while desperately trying to keep his fucking fingers out of my ass. He was gentleman enough to drive me home the next morning, which is more than I can say for most.

Of course Daniel found out. I wish it had been Tim's slipup, but it was mine. That's when he stopped speaking to me. I was so angry with him at the time. Thought he was blowing it completely out of proportion. Being a giant fucking whining baby. But he wasn't. He was completely justified.

I was a dumb slut.

I am a dumb slut. Present tense.

By the time I get to Avenue B I'm starting to come down already. I remember when pills could keep me going for ten-hour stretches. And the comedown was half the fun. A day of coffee, pajamas, and children's television. Now I hate comedowns. I'm fucking exhausted. I light a cigarette on the corner of B and Fourteenth, and it feels like chewing a mouthful of ash. I let it dangle at my side until it burns down to the filter and the heat pinches my fingertips. I flick it into the street as I come up to Jason's building.

What the fuck was the code again?

Upstairs the apartment is dark. Gray light filtering through the permanent dust on the tiny kitchen window. The door to Jason's room is closed. I bet Train Station Boy is in there. I collapse on the love seat and switch on a table lamp. I turn the TV on and change it to the Discovery Channel. Something about space. Anything to stave off the thoughts my serotonin-depleted brain will undoubtedly produce. About how numb I feel.

I wake to Jason sitting in the chair opposite me, ripping a typically enormous bong hit. I feel like someone's been stabbing me in the head while I was asleep. It's dark out.

"Oh, I am going to be a *bitch* today." I sit up slowly. My insides feel fragile, like crystal. I may shatter.

"I think you mean tonight. Here. Hit this." Jay hands me the bong.

"That's what I like to hear." I take a steady, methodical hit and exhale carefully.

"How many pills did you take?"

"Three."

"Well, don't even think about taking your comedown out on me."

"So compassionate."

"Hey, you did this to yourself. Besides, I'm in a great mood today."

"I'll bet Train Station Boy saw to that."

"Why, yes he did. Thank you for that, by the way. You must've got some?"

"No, I got some. It was just . . . pointless."

"And what, pray tell, was the last thing *you* thought had a point?" He's got a point there. "That's too bad— Jesse's hot."

Jesse. That's his name.

"It just didn't do anything for me. I couldn't get into it. I was too, I don't know . . ."

"Conscious?"

"Cripplingly self-aware."

"Now *that's* the title of your autobiography. Hands down."

"When did I stop enjoying enjoyable things?"

"Damned if I know. I'm not sure I can ever remember you enjoying anything in the first place . . . not really."

"Fair enough. This conversation is taking a turn for the depressing, so I'm going to change the subject."

"To what?"

"Why, to you of course."

"Ooh, my favorite."

"What did you tell him?" I shake my thumb at Jay's bedroom door.

"Who? Train Station Boy?"

"Yeah."

"Staff photographer for *Rolling Stone*. Old standby. Oh, and I'm in a band."

"Called?"

"Winter Star in the Morning."

"Ooh, emo, I like it."

"I had a hard time saying it without laughing."

"No you didn't."

"Fair enough."

It's late when I decide to grab a train back to Philly. I walk to the subway trying to figure out what day it is, which means trying to recount when this most recent bender actually began. Well, I definitely remember drinks in the 'Vous with Kat was Wednesday night, because she met me after work. But I was certainly out somewhere Monday and Tuesday as well, and most probably over the weekend before that. So, was the party in West Philly on Thursday? No, that was Friday. Shit, what did I do Thursday?

I can't remember.

Friday was the party with Cocaine Boy, brunch with Jason on Saturday. Was the Brooklyn party the same night or the next? No, it was still Saturday. So today is . . . Sunday.

Fuck. I may have been set free from the café, but I still have to open the bar tomorrow.

By the time I'm in Philadelphia, sitting on the Broad Street Line, heading toward Lombard Street, my come-down is in full swing. The lights on the train are glaring, slicing my eyes. I close them. I have a Snapple bottle that's half filled with Jim Beam and ginger ale that Jay gave me for the trip home, and I swig out of that. The smell of my breath reminds me of Daniel. All those nights he'd come to bed after dawn and yawn and nuzzle against me, humid Beam-breath in my face. It used to make me sick to my stomach. Now it makes me sad. I think about the last night we spent in the North Philly house together, when I told him I couldn't do it anymore. I didn't cry. Just spoke really sternly and rationally. Like a schoolteacher. It was so hot that night and it was only May. Neither of us moved, just lay naked on top of the covers and talked and sweated. We both knew we'd fucked it all up, or that I had, but he still wasn't willing to give up on it. On me. So I had to be the one who gave up on him. He went to his parents' the next day.

Then I cried.

Like a fucking child.

Remembering now makes my nose sting and my chest tighten. Don't cry. You know it was the right thing to do. It was the right thing to do it was the right thing to do-it-was-the-right-thing-to-doitwastherightthingtodo.

I think.

I hate comedowns.

I wipe a few hot tears from under my eyes with my filthy sleeve.

It's just the drugs. The drugs are making you feel this way.

It's late, I think. There's no one around. The only other person in the car is an older man. Well, older than me.

He's wearing a long dark coat that it's not cold enough for. Navy or black, I can never tell. I don't think he's tall, and his nose reminds me of my dad's. Roman. His hair is dark and graying at the temples. Salt-and-pepper, my mom would've called it. Distinguished.

He's sitting across the aisle from me, reading a worn paperback. I have to strain to read the title because the cover is faded and creased. And my eyes won't focus.

A Handful of Dust.

I read that sophomore year of college, in that class I took with Daniel. Modern British Fiction. I loved that book. Love that book. Present tense.

Fuck, who wrote it?

I squint harder at the cover, but he looks up and sees me. Shit. I must look like a complete crazy person. I look out the window as my face burns, but all I see is black, and me looking back, reflected in the Plexiglas. Like an underdeveloped photo. A ghost image. My forehead is shiny, and my hair's greasy. I look like a street urchin. Sallow, like something out of Dickens.

I picture him staring at the back of my head. Brows furrowed. Concerned. He probably thinks I'm sixteen. A runaway. A whore. What if he propositions me? I wonder how much it'd take for me to go down on this stranger, in this train car, right now. Five hundred bucks? Two fifty? What if I propositioned *him*? He's decent-looking.

Suck your cock for fifty bucks.

There's something appealing about that idea. And I could certainly use fifty bucks. I imagine sliding in beside him, putting my hand on his thigh. Feeling the muscles jump at an unexpected touch. Looking up at him. You wanna go somewhere? I imagine him getting hard. Thinking to himself, *no, I would never,* but finding himself incredibly attracted to how pathetic I am, turned on by his own pity.

I'd tell him my name was Lola . . . Dolores . . . Dolly.

I peek over my shoulder at him and he's reading.

He's not thinking anything about me.

When the train stops at Walnut/Locust he gets off and heads toward the PATCO line. He's going to Jersey. My stop is next, but just as the doors start to close, I spring up and out onto the platform. I convince myself at first that I'm gonna walk the extra two blocks home, but really I'm going back to Jersey.

It would be good to see Mom, anyway.

As I turn through the underground hallways, following red PATCO signs, I can hear echoes of his footsteps around corners ahead of me. By the time I get to the platform, he is sitting on a bench in the center. Reading again.

I still can't make out the author.

I walk to the edge of the platform and turn my back to him. I want him to be watching me. I light a cigarette and then swig some of my faux Snapple peach iced tea, holding the cigarette between the first and middle fingers of the hand gripping the bottle, because it looks cooler than using two hands. I try to stand nonchalantly but find myself hunched awkwardly.

Waugh. Evelyn fucking Waugh.

When the train comes I let him get on ahead of me, and I sit at the opposite end of the car from him. It's such a cliché, but there's something about him. What am I doing? Am I following someone? Have I sunk this low?

Oh well. I certainly have nothing better to do.

I'm just going to stay at Mom's anyway. I do that sometimes. That's acceptable. If I happen to find out what stop he gets off at on my way, so be it.

I want to know his name.

The train takes me back across the river to New Jersey, only much farther south this time. I hope, as we approach the Walter Rand Transportation Center where I'll have to transfer to the Riverline, that he'll get off before me, and then I'll know something. I'll know something about him.

I'll know his stop.

But he doesn't get off. He stays on the train. And now I'm in Jersey.

Fuck.

As I leave the station, what is probably the last River-line train of the night is heading toward the platform opposite me. The train is sleek and small, just installed this past summer. It looks out of place here. The streets behind the platform are littered with garbage and poor people. Poor black people. Pushed into the wasteland of urban sprawl and left to rot.

I always thought cramped and poor Upper Darby, where I grew up, was bad. Full of narrow stucco twins and even narrower row homes. And I always knew New Jersey was crap. But once I moved out and Mom moved to the Garden State, I realized that I don't just hate New Jersey the way everyone from Philadelphia and New York generically "hates" New Jersey.

I fucking hate fucking New fucking Jersey.

My phone is dead so I have to walk from the Delanco stop to Mom's new house. There's no sidewalk on this stretch, and no streetlights either, but seeing as how it's well past one in the morning, I don't see any cars. I can see the edge of the development after only a few minutes.

It's massive and right smack in the center of East Bum-blefuck. On one side, clinical greenspace, on the other, trucking companies. I could walk all the way around it, to the front entrance and then back through the winding quiet streets to where Mom's house sits against the edge of the property line. But I won't. Instead, I cut across the sloping backyards belonging to other white middle-class retirees. It cuts the walk in half and involves only minor trespassing.

The houses all look alike. So do the cars in the driveways, and all the front porches.

McMansions. Squat and pale. Slapped together with clapboard and drywall. Fronted with faux stone or vinyl siding. Brand spanking new, identical black mailboxes stand on the curbs like soldiers in a line, each with its own bright red flag to wave and ordered numerical identity.

I pledge allegience. . . .

When I finally find soldier number 87 I try the front door and it's open. Typical. On the first floor of the house, there are no walls dividing the rooms, only square wooden supports. From the front entrance I can see into all the rooms on the floor, sans Mom's bedroom. The office, dining room, and front hall are all dark, but a blue glow seeps around the corner of the living room into the kitchen. And the mumble of the TV. I hope it's Mom up and not Jim. There's no way to know. They're both raging insomniacs. I listen for the TV. If it's sports I'm heading right upstairs.

Shit, I can't tell.

I'll risk it.

As I turn the corner I see the top of Mom's dark head above the back of her chair. Blue smoke halos her. Thank god. I cannot deal with Jim right now.

No matter how gently I try to announce my arrival, I will undoubtedly scare the shit out of her. There is no way to do it without startling her. I put my hand on the top of her head.

"Mom?"

She turns sharply in her chair, hand to chest, and gasps.

"Alright Scarlett O'Hara, no need to be so dramatic."

"Jesus Christ, you scared the shit out of me." She smacks my upper arm.

"Sorry." I come into the room and sit on the bright purple couch next to her. It's buried in plump, brightly colored pillows. I have to shove piles of them to the floor to make room for myself.

"What are you doing in Stepford?"

"Feeling shit. Can I stay the night?"

"Of course, sweetie. You know you can always stay.

Just don't leave a damn mess around. Suli just cleaned today."

"I thought she came on Fridays so you could have the house clean for the weekend." I take a cigarette from her pack on the table and light it.

"Well, this week I pushed it to Sunday because I took off work on Friday and I wanted to sit around in my underwear and eat Cheetos and watch TV."

"Learned any Portuguese yet?"

"No. It's fucking difficult."

"Fair enough."

"Where've you been?"

"New York."

"How's Jason doing?"

"He's alright." I lay my hand across my eyes and lean back into the couch.

"You guys partying? You look like you had a rough weekend."

"Try a rough two weeks." I pull my legs up onto the couch and curl them into me. Fetal.

"Honey, I hope you're being safe."

"I guess that depends on your definition of safe."

"Why've you been hitting it so hard recently? Something going on? And speaking of hitting it hard, why haven't you packed a bowl yet?"

"Good call." I dig two small plastic containers of weed out of my bag and hand her one. "This is yours. It's that really strong stuff Jay's roommate gets that really fucks you up, so be careful with it." I crack mine open and break off a nug for the bowl.

I hit it and pass it to her. "I'm alright I guess. I mean, I don't know, I'm just bored."

"Bored?"

"Well, yeah, or . . . disinterested."

"In what?"

"Everything." I snort a laugh.

"Are you taking your meds?"

"I guess that depends on your definition of meds."

Her head flops over on her shoulder and she furrows her brow at me. "Very cute. You know what I mean."

"I don't like them, Mom. They make me . . . cloudy."

"So try new ones—"

"That's just it"—she hates when I interrupt her—"I don't want to just keep taking different medication, hoping someday one might possibly make me feel, slightly, sorta better. They make me feel like ass—I'm not taking them."

"What about the panic attacks?"

"I haven't had any." But I can feel them lurking in my head and my gut. Like worms waiting to devour me.

"Fine." She's gonna change the subject. "Have you talked to Daniel recently?"

"No. You know he doesn't want to talk to me."

"It's just such a shame. You two . . . I don't know, it just seemed to make sense."

"Yes, I know, thank you. It was perfect and I'm a big dumb fuck up who pushed away the only decent man that will ever love me . . . blah blah blah."

"You know I don't think that, Ms. Sensitive."

"Sorry. I've just been thinking about him a lot recently. He's been popping into my head." To remind me how badly I fucked it up by being a completely absurd human.

"You think that's why you're feeling like shit?"

"No, but it certainly hasn't helped. It's more just that nothing's fun. Everything sucks. Everyone's lame. God, that makes me sound so *boring*."

"Well, honey, if you're so against taking your meds—"

"Mom, let it go."

"Fine. Donna suggested exercise and meditation."

"I really don't see that happening, Mom. It's not me."

"So what is you? Being miserable?" She has a point there.

"It would seem so."

"I guarantee those things would make you feel better."

"I guarantee they wouldn't. What am I gonna do? Jog? Swim? That's hideous. And meditation? I'm in my own head quite enough as it is, and I don't much like it, to be honest." I punctuate my point by stabbing out the butt of my pilfered Camel Turkish Silver. "In fact, that's probably my biggest problem."

"Alright fine. What can I do?"

"Nothing, Mom. It's alright. Really." I hate to make her feel obsolete, because she's definitely not. "Let me bum another cigarette?"

"You smoke way too much." She sits in her usual chair. Wrapped in a yellow comforter. It was mine when I was a kid. It used to have a cover with purple and white hearts on it. It followed us from house to house. Now she uses it for a different kind of comfort. It's become her blankie. She misses me. Four-year-old me. The me that snuggled up with her and read *The Runaway Bunny*. The me that loved the purple and white hearts. The me that entertained her endlessly. Better than this me that scares her. That worries her. That she has no control over.

"Be a prancing dear and get the ice cream. And two spoons."

I groan even though I know I'm going to do it.

"Don't groan. You have young legs."

"You sound like Paw-paw."

"I know. I'm old and decrepit."

"Shut up." I hate when she says stuff like that. I get up and head to the kitchen.

In the freezer there are no less than three pints of ice cream. Two Ben & Jerry's, one Häagen-Dazs.

"Which do you want?" I yell through to her. I know it was too loud. I don't care.

"Shh. Jim's sleeping."

"Whatever."

"What is there?"

"Phish Food from the last time I was here. An unopened pint of Half Baked and some coffee Häagen-Dazs."

"Ooh, Häagen-Dazs. Yeah." She claps her hands together excitedly and kicks her chair with the heels of her bare feet, which don't touch the carpet.

I bring in the coffee and the Phish Food and two massive spoons. We sit silently, staring at the TV, scooping giant mouthfuls of ice cream. My hand is freezing and I pull my sleeve over it. My tongue is numb.

"Are you going to work tomorrow morning?" I pass her the bowl, freshly packed, and toss her a lighter.

"Yeah, I think so. You need a ride?"

"Yeah, I have to be at the bar at, like, 10:30."

"Yeah, no problem. We can leave at quarter to ten. But why don't you just call out? Hang out here."

"Well, I can't really afford to. I got fired from the café yesterday."

"Why?"

"For calling out too much."

"Are you gonna be OK for cash?"

"Yeah, I think so."

"Well, let me know if you need any help. I can't give you a ton, but I'm sure I can find something."

"Thanks. It's fine, really."

"What time is it anyway?"

"It's three."

"In the morning? Shit. I'm off to bed." She hands me the bowl and the lighter. "Good night, sweetheart. Don't stay up too late—try and get some sleep. You'll feel better."

"I will." I won't.

"Oh, and I think *maybe* you should at least *think* about *maybe* calling Daniel."

"Why?"

"I don't like you two not talking. You should at least be friends after everything."

"I don't know. Maybe." I don't care. "I don't really care. Friends, not friends, what's the difference? It doesn't matter. He can hate me if he wants. He has the right."

Even I hate me. Why should I begrudge him the same?

"I'm sure he doesn't hate you."

I'm sure he does. "I don't know. I'll think about it. Go to bed."

"I'm going." Her round pink face peers out of the mass of comforter that surrounds her as she gets up and pads into her bedroom. "Good night, Baby Bear."

"Good night, Mama Bear."

54

I'm not tired. My body is wrecked, but I'm not tired. I should take a shower. I haven't had a shower since I fucked Fire Escape Boy, and I want to scrub him off me.

I throw my bag on the bed in the downstairs guest room. In the bathroom I stand in front of the sink and realize that this is the first time I've seen a mirror in over twenty-four hours.

Oh Jesus.

Is that the face I'm using to represent myself? No wonder people keep giving me drugs. I look like a heroin addict.

My eyes aren't just bloodshot, the entire whites are now pinks. They squint painfully back at themselves. My pupils are pinpricks under the bathroom fluorescents. Irises: muddy green and fogged over. Clumps of dull hair snake over my shoulders. Matted and tangled. My face is shining greasily. Blackheads sprout on my nose and chin. I pull on the saggy blue-black half circles that hang from my eye sockets. Lips: predictably dry and cracked, painful with incessant gurning. I curl my lips, exposing my teeth. Yellow and weak-looking, like they might just up and decide to crumble out of my head. The thought makes my gums hurt. Tongue: white and sticky. Breath: horrendous.

I turn the shower all the way to hot and undress as the room fills with steam. Just before I get in, I turn it just a touch to cold, so it's still painful, but just bearable. I stand under the spray, watching my skin start glowing red. I wash everything. Twice. I take my time.

When I get out there's a big, dry, clean towel on the rack.

It's nice to be at Mom's.

I brush my teeth and tongue. I gag.

In the guest room I lie naked on top of the covers. Daniel is creeping in the corners of my consciousness. Begging to be dealt with.

That horrible day when I found his journal. Why did I open it? It's like I was looking for something to validate my fears that someone so sane and wonderful couldn't possibly be honestly interested in me. I was convinced he was jerking me around. And then, dumb fuck that I am, I read his journal. "Sometimes I want to marry her, and sometimes I can't stand to be around her." It was the last thing I expected.

The truth.

The one he wanted to marry, that was the real me. I know it. Deep down, that was me. Fun, smart, outgoing. The one he couldn't stand, that was the scared me. The paranoid, depressed me that was slowly but surely taking over. I couldn't stop it. Couldn't stop the one from consuming the other. And he could see it.

But he woulda stuck it out. Taken the bad with the good and all that bullshit.

Me? I made his life miserable for three years and then broke his heart.

We stopped having sex when I was so far in a hole that my sex drive switched itself off completely. He thought it was him. At the time, I thought it was him. But it wasn't. It was me.

It's not you, it's me.

There should be a word for a truthful cliché.

A truché.

He thought he could make me happy, but I just made him depressed. Three years of dealing with me would bring anyone down.

This is stupid. This is so fucking stupid. What is wrong with me?

How long have I been this? It feels like forever.

I don't want to think about this anymore.

I dig around in my head for something else. Something without association. Something detached. Something I can enjoy thinking about.

The man on the train. The Stranger on a Train. I picture the whole train car, empty except for us. I see myself. I look younger, disheveled, svelte. Played by Thora Birch circa *American Beauty*. He's solid, dark. A strand of hair hangs in his eyes. And then I do it. Something I could never really do. I slide in next to him, put my hand on his book and lower it to his lap. I look into his face and push the stray hairs back, running my fingers gently along his graying temple. He looks down at me. Stern. I smile. Kittenish. That's what I want to be, kittenish. I climb up into his lap, straddle him. He drops his book.

Imagining it, I slide my naked body between the crisp sheets. I let my wet head rest in the overstuffed pillows. They smell clean.

I cradle his face in my hands and tilt it upward. He's stunned. Complicit. I lean in and kiss him slowly, sucking on his upper lip. Biting. His hand comes up and rests on my waist. He's kissing me back.

In bed, I run my hand down my body, under the covers. I ignore my breasts and slide my palm between my legs. I press it sideways between my thighs and warm my fingers.

He slides his hand under my shirt, along my ribs. A thick, calloused thumb brushes the underside of my breast, small and pale against his hand.

It's not the thought of him touching me, but the thought of him wanting to touch me that turns me on.

I move gently against my middle finger. My eyes are closed. If I stop. If I think. About clit, finger, pubic hair, fingernails, this room, this bed.

Then I'll ruin it.

So I won't.

Instead, I think about my hands on his belt buckle.

Slowly pulling the strap back, the buckle forward. I think about pleasing him. I fantasize about being his fantasy. I kneel in the train; cold metal digs at my knees. My jeans are gone. I suck him off while looking up into his face. I watch the way he responds, the faces he makes when he doesn't realize I'm watching him. I'm in control of his pleasure. It makes me want to fuck him.

I'm getting somewhere. Getting wet. I keep my pace steady, slowly building momentum. An orgasm takes a lot of careful maneuvering. I don't want to lose this one.

I'm back on top of him, straddling. He's fully clothed, coat still on, pants pulled down only as much as they need to be for me to slide onto his cock.

Imagining the thick pressure of him inside me takes me up a notch, and I press harder, rub my clit just that much faster.

I'm completely naked, hands clutching his chest, picking up speed. Rocking him in and out of me. I lean in and kiss him, grabbing handfuls of dark, sleek hair. I'm doing this for him. I'm not going to cum in this fantasy, but he certainly is. I look in his eyes and make sure it's very clear to him that I'm about to *give* him an orgasm. And that's what it is, a gift.

And for one second, I'm there.

In the moment.

There's nothing.

No train, no mysterious stranger, no guest bed-room, no crisp sheets. Just me and my orgasm.

My back arches. I gasp slightly. I shudder.

I open my eyes and exhale.

Jesus, even my fantasies are pathetic. I should write cheap romance novels.

Driving down 130 South in the morning, Mom and I pass no less than six Dunkin' Donuts in the course of a thirty-minute drive. We stop at a McDonald's drive-thru and get McMuffins and orange juice. It's greasy and plastic and tastes ridiculously good.

I can't go home and change 'cause the fast-food stop made us late. I can't get away with being late. Again. Aidan gets so pompous about that shit.

It's making me anxious. I want to yell at my mom. Tell her to speed the fuck up, but I can't.

Besides, fuck Aidan.

As we cross the Betsy Ross Bridge I light two ciga-rettes and pass one to Mom. The raw-sewage smell of factory waste is stifling.

"You look a bit better this morning."

Do I? "Yeah, I needed some sleep, I guess."

Once we're over the bridge and into Center City, the smell changes to car exhaust and warm garbage. Mom pulls up at Walnut and Twentieth and lets me out.

"Thanks." I kiss her on the cheek through her window.

"I love you, honey. Have a good day."

I watch her Camry pull through the light and down the street before I light another cigarette and head around the back alley to the bar's kitchen entrance. I'm ten minutes late. Aidan better not get all fucking smart with me.

Jefe the cook sits on the back steps, smoking. He looks up as I turn the corner and shrugs at me.

Aidan's not here yet. Asshole. He's supposed to be here at 9:30 to open the bar. I don't have keys. Jefe hands me his phone with Aidan's number on the screen, ready to call. Jefe doesn't speak any English.

It rings for ages and then goes to voice mail. I call again.

"Hmm, yes?"

"Aidan, get up."

"What?"

"Aidan, it's 10:45 and the bar's not open yet."

"Oh shit. Be there in ten."

I hang up and sit on the step next to Jefe. I hand him his phone back.

"Diez minutos."

Jefe shrugs.

Twenty-five minutes later Aidan lets us in. At this point I'm just glad that's twenty-five minutes less I have to work.

I set the tables, make coffee, and sit at the end of the bar, staring at *The Philadelphia Inquirer*'s crossword puzzle. No one's gonna come in today. I may be making two dollars an hour to sit on my ass and smoke cigarettes, but my rent's $650 a month.

Aidan yammers at me from behind the bar in his only slightly Americanized Irish accent. Something about getting some drunk girls to get their tits out at the bar last night. He's wearing a T-shirt that says "Drink 'til she's Irish."

"I took two of 'em home."

I'm not even acknowledging that he's talking.

"Giant tits, man. Huge." He's squeezing his own invisible breasts. Lolling his tongue like some mangy dog.

"You really are the pinnacle of class, Aidan."

"You know why I like living in America? The girls all shave their pubes. I bet you do."

"You know, I thought we had enough assholes here already, but apparently we have to import them now."

"You're not wearing a bra are you?"

"Fuck off, don't even think about it."

"Come on. I've been wanting to get a look at your tits since the day you started working here. Get 'em out, let me get my hands on 'em."

"Never fucking happen."

"Come on, you know you think I'm cute. And if my

time in the States has taught me anything, it's that this accent is a fucking open sesame."

He is cute. And the accent is just unfair. These dumb, pathetic undergrads don't stand a chance. Thank god I'm immune to cocky-asshole-itis. "You're right, I just can't keep my hands off you."

"Oh, sarcasm. There's a new one for you."

"It's a speech impediment. Everything I say sounds sarcastic."

"I've noticed."

By the afternoon the only person to come in is the Postman. The Postman comes in every morning, in uniform, with a bag full of mail. He sits at the bar and drinks four Bombay martinis. He insists on watching CNN, and he tips Aidan a dollar in quarters every time. Sometimes he puts Tony Bennett on the jukebox. Aidan hates the Postman.

Sometimes I hate the Postman and sometimes I feel sorry for him. Today I don't care.

Around two the door opens. Looking up from my still unstarted crossword, I feel my organs tense.

No fucking way. What is he doing here?

The Stranger on a Train.

Like I've said, small town posing as a big city. He must work in the city, he's on his lunch break. Maybe he even lives here. I just assumed he lived in Jersey. Has he been in before? Have I walked past him a hundred times? What made me suddenly notice him?

I can't help but flash back to my fantasy. His hand on my hip, mine in his hair. My cheeks are hot, and I know I'm blushing. I stub out my half-finished cigarette and approach him.

"Hi. How you doing today?"

"Fine. Just one for lunch, please." His voice is soft.

"Smoking"—I gesture to the empty front of house—"or non?"—and the empty back. I want to make a joke about the place being empty. Something about how it doesn't matter where he sits or smokes because there's no one to be bothered by it. But I can't get my word choice together quickly enough.

"Smoking."

I lead him to a table in the back and lay a menu in front of him.

"Can I get you a drink?" I picture myself asking him the same thing inside the door of my apartment. Or not my apartment, a nicer, cleaner apartment.

"What do you have on tap?"

I try to do it without turning around and looking at the bar.

"Miller Lite, Magic Hat #9, Stella, Boddingtons . . . um, Guinness . . ." Shit there's at least three more.

"Guinness is fine, thanks."

Saved.

When I pick his drink up from the bar, my palms and upper lip are sweaty. I wipe my hands on my jeans and run the back of my hand across my mouth. Aidan leers at me.

"What's the matter with you?"

"What do you mean? I'm fine."

"You're usually a total bitch to customers. You're actually being polite to this guy."

"Isn't it obvious? I'm desperately trying to impress you with my service abilities."

"I thought so."

Why *do* I care? What's making me so nervous? I don't even know this guy.

But I want to.

There's something so calm about him. He's sitting there, so settled.

So settled in himself.

My hand shakes and I have to use both to set his pint down.

"What can I get you to eat?" I look down at him. He glances up and makes eye contact. He has heartbreaking eyelashes. For a moment I think he recognizes me. Maybe he noticed me on the train, too. Maybe he jacked off thinking about me.

He glances back down at the menu.

"Um, just a cheeseburger."

I'm aware of my dirty shirt, my free-swinging boobs, my slumping shoulders. I try to stand up straight and it hurts. Something in my back makes a cracking noise.

"How would you like that cooked?"

"Medium."

Why does this hideously demeaning exchange have to be our first?

"Fries or salad?"

"Salad."

"Great. Won't be long."

I go in the back and enter the order in the computer. I want to stab forks in my eyes. Could I have a lamer existence? Why is this me?

I deliver his food and get him a second Guinness without looking at him. I sit at the far end of the bar and suck a cigarette. Hunched over the paper, I refuse to glance behind at him. I refuse to think about him looking at me. And I *certainly* refuse to think about him *not* looking at me.

I stare through the paper in front of me, through the bar under it, through the sink and the pipes and the basement. Through dirt and dark. I flash forward.

We're in a sunny kitchen. Him and me. The table

we're sitting at is round and bright pine. A vase with one tulip. We're drinking coffee and reading the paper. He's reading the reviews and I'm doing the cryptogram. I'm older, my hair thick and wavy. The tiny, faint creases that frame my eyes and mouth are in direct contrast to the dark bold strokes that carve his face. We're both smoking, and I pull my knee up under my chin. Played by Sandra Bullock wearing a bulky sweater. *While You Were Sleeping*, maybe.

Why does this man make me think in clichés?

Aidan drags me out of my future by pulling my hair.

"I think your man is done."

"He can wait."

"Now that's more like it."

I clear his plate and he's smoking a Marlboro Red. Guinness, red meat, and Cowboy Killers. No wonder I like him.

"Anything else I can get for you?"

"Another Guinness."

I lean on the bar, watching his pint settle. What if I just walked over there, sat down, and introduced myself? What if I said, "I saw you on the train. You were reading *A Handful of Dust*. One of my favorites," and then asked his name. Stuck out my hand and told him my own?

Because I'm his waitress and that's weird. Because I just spent half an hour serving him. Asking him deep, personal questions about his eating preferences. I'm not real to him. As soon as he walks out that door, I vanish.

When I bring him his drink, I linger, pathetically. My hand on the back of the chair across from him. I can see myself pulling it out, sitting confidently. Bumming a cigarette. Elbows on the table.

My shift's done at seven, buy me a drink?

How would he respond?

I realize he's staring at me. My mouth opens, uselessly. I touch my lips with my fingertips.

"I'll just get your check."

I take one of his beers off the check. Maybe he'll pay with a credit card—then I'll know his name.

He pays in cash. Tips me five bucks, which is almost 30 percent. The last true gentleman.

My head spins a little when he's gone. Like he wasn't really there at all. Like my deluded brain made him up to keep itself occupied. To give it something better to do than pick itself apart.

Kat comes in when my shift's over, and I'm still shaken up. For the last couple of hours I've been having flashes. The Stranger and I out to dinner. Him meeting my mother. Our two bodies tangled in bedclothes and

each other, sleeping with our foreheads pressed together. Me smiling. Laughing even.

I'm startled when Kat sits at the bar next to me.
She's singing.

I've got Pabst Blue Ribbon on my mind.
I've got Pabst Blue Ribbon on my mind.
The change under the sofa's all the money I could find.
I've got Pabst Blue Ribbon on my mind!

"Hmm, I wonder what you want to do tonight."

"What's the matter with you? You look like you got
punched in the stomach."

"What? Nothing. Rough weekend."

"Yeah, where the fuck were you? You went MIA
Friday night."

"That party sucked. I went to New York and stayed
with Jay."

"Who's jealous? Me. Why didn't you tell me? I'd
have come too."

"Sorry. It was really last-minute. I just had to get
out of there. Anyway, my phone's dead."

"Yeah well, let's go to the 'Vous and get shitfaced.
How much money you got on you?"

"Five to my name."

"Perfect. I stole two bucks from the kitchen table in
Chipmunk's house. I bet we manage to get trashed on
seven tonight."

"We do always seem to manage."

"Aidan!" Kat calls as we're leaving, "I'm already Irish."

On the street: "Don't encourage him. If his ego was any bigger he'd be . . . well, he'd be you."

"He's an amateur."

"You should have an ego-off."

"Are you kidding? I would destroy. Anyway, he's gorgeous. I would totally bone that."

"And you could. He's a breast man. And those things you're hauling around are damn near ridiculous."

"They come in handy."

"I feel sorry for your boyfriend."

"What he doesn't know won't, blah, blah, blah. Anyway, you don't even like Ben."

"You're right. Forget I said anything. I'm well aware that you're a serial cheater. A leopard can't change its spots."

"And nor should it want to, my friend. And nor should it want to."

"Hey, I salute you. I'm not emotionally stable enough to keep one relationship going, let alone juggle three or four. Or ten. How many have you got going these days?"

"Like I can keep track. The key is honestly not caring if they find out."

"So the key is actually not liking any of them?"

"Probably."

If life were food, Kat's would be candy.

When we get to the Locust Rendezvous Kat searches the after-work drinkers for her targets. She's an experienced con artist. She convinces pathetic men that one or both of us might sleep with them if they continually buy us drinks throughout the evening. It's the only way we can afford to sit in bars all night. Whether she actually does sleep with them or not is a direct result of how much booze she's had, multiplied by how attractive they are. Whether I do or not depends directly on the ratio between my self-esteem level at the time, and the guy's. But shit, who am I to turn down a free drink?

She's not particularly beautiful. She's little, big-chested, and vulgar. This makes her attractive to lonely thirtysomething computer programmers. She also smokes a lot of reefer and listens to the Grateful Dead. This makes her attractive to nouveau hippies and frat boys, which comes in handy in a college town. They line up at the bar to buy her drinks. She's good to have around. I can't be asked to put in the effort.

Sitting at our usual booth in the Locust Rendezvous, she lights two cigarettes and hands one to me.

"So what the fuck is wrong with you today? You look . . . distracted. Well, even more so than usual."

"I don't know. This guy came in."

"Ooh, what guy? Cute guy?"

"No. Well, kinda. Not cute, that's not the point."

"What is the point?"

"I don't know. I saw him on the train this weekend, and he just . . . like, stuck with me."

"And then he came into the bar today?"

"Yeah."

"I hate this fucking one-horse town. There are, like, eight people in it and they've all fucked each other."

"Just 'cause you can't sneeze without blowing snot on someone who 'blew their snot' on you . . ." I make quotation marks in the air with my fingers.

"You know what I mean. Remember that hot guy who worked at Stellar and always gave you free coffee?"

"God, I saw him everywhere. Never managed to get boned though. Wonder what happened to him anyway. Haven't seen him around in ages."

"Maybe he managed the practically impossible feat of getting the hell out of Dodge."

"Lucky son of a bitch. But this guy, I've never seen him before and then, bang, twice in two days."

"What's so special about him that he's got your panties all twisted?"

"Nothing. I don't know. He's older. He was reading a book I really like."

"How much older?"

"Dunno. Forty-five? Fifty maybe?"

"Hello, Grandpa. Is he married?"

"How the fuck should I know? It's not like I fucking interrogated the man—he's a complete stranger." He better fucking not be married. "It never even occurred to me."

"A married man is a dangerous thing."

"Never stops you."

"And this is why I know."

By the time our pitcher is dry, Kat's invited two Penn med students into our booth, Blond Loser and Short Loser. Also known as Bro and Dude.

I hate Penn students.

Spoiled, rich kids. All of 'em. Good targets, however, thanks to Daddy's credit card. If you can stand to listen to them speak.

And boy do they love slumming it.

After a few pitchers and a lifetime of boring conversation, Blond Loser stands up and takes his wallet out of his back pocket.

"Hey, I'm going to the bar. You girls ready for another pitcher?"

"Hell yes." Kat pipes up, enthusiastic as ever.

"Hey Bro, get me a Stella this time," Short Loser commands his comrade. And then an aside, meant for my and Kat's benefit, I assume, "I spent a semester in Europe."

"They don't have Stella." I'm being particularly cold. I'm just not in the mood for this shit. I can't play the game. Besides, I'll get the drinks either way. Kat'll keep getting pitchers, and Short Loser is not giving up on her. No matter how much of an ice queen I am.

"Oh right. Well, a Guinness then."

"No dice, buddy."

Kat glares at me. Short Loser is a bit knocked off his game. All I can think about is whether or not there was a ring. I saw his hands, I'm sure of it. Was there a ring?

"Budweiser?" He raises his eyebrows at me. I want to snatch them off his face.

"Now he's learning." I light a cigarette and give one to Kat to make amends.

Blond Loser sits back down and tops up our glasses.

"Dude, come outside for a cigarette with me." He jerks his head at Short Loser.

"You can smoke in here, Bro."

"Just come outside for a minute, Dude."

Once they're outside Kat leans across the table to me.

"Yours is cuter. Let's swap."

"Take 'em both."

"You could stand to cheer the fuck up. I certainly don't want to go home sober tonight, and unless you're gonna start pulling gold ducats out of your ass, this is our only meal ticket."

I look outside. The Losers are talking sternly. Mine doesn't look happy. He doesn't like me. Yet for some reason I can picture this night ending with me wrestling his meaty paws off some part of my anatomy.

"I'm not fucking him."

"Fine. Don't. What do I care? Just don't be such a hideous bitch."

"But I'm so good at it."

I used to be able to flirt. I used to like it. I flirted in high school, I flirted with Daniel. And after being with him for about a year, I flirted hard, with anyone. It wasn't even to make him jealous. It was to make me feel good. It wasn't enough that one man wanted me, I had to have them all after me. His friends, my friends, strangers in bars. I never cheated, I don't think. But I might as well have. I was never the best-looking girl in the room, but I was certainly the most accessible. Even while I was doing it I knew it was all a pathetic attempt to marginally raise my self-esteem for a minimal period of time.

And honestly, at the time, even that minor, temporary boost was worth it.

Now, I can't even be fucked to put the effort in.

When the boys slide back in the booth, Short Loser leans in conspiratorially.

"You girls wouldn't be interested in a little pick-me-up, would you?"

Oh god, am I in a bad eighties movie?

"Yes!" More enthusiasm from Kat.

"What do you mean by 'pick-me-up' exactly?" What I want to say to the douche bag is this, The code talk is real hip and all, but I don't want to end up in some kind of K-hole and I'm pretty sure the two bull dykes making out behind us aren't undercover DEA agents, so why don't you tell *us* what the guy who sold you that depressing mix of baby aspirin and diet pills *claimed* he was selling you. But I know Kat would probably punch me in the tit.

"Well, we got a little blow . . ."

Jesus! What is with this? I can't decide if the drug gods are blessing or punishing me. Will I constantly be supplied with various narcotics at appropriate moments throughout my entire life? Or will I die here, in this dive bar, tonight? On the floor of the ladies' room. Ajax burning a hole through my gray matter.

When will my luck run out?

Fuck it.

"We're interested."

The Losers each go to the men's room, passing the little plastic Baggie under the table. Slick. Then Short Loser hands it to Kat, who nods at me. Being a girl makes doing drugs in public places so much easier. We can go together. Share with some level of privacy. We have stalls, with doors that lock.

In the bathroom I straddle the toilet seat backward, cutting lines on the top of the tank. On the wall in front of me, some undiscovered poet has scrawled CUNT into the dirty paint.

"Make 'em big ones. Fatties."

"What the fuck did you think I was gonna do? Not do that?" We're giggling. Gleeful at having pulled off such a massive score. These guys think they're *definitely* getting laid now. But now we don't need them. We got what we wanted.

They have over three-quarters of a gram left, and we cane most of it in four fat lines.

"Oh. This." Sniff. "Is really nice stuff."

"Rich kids are certainly good for something."

There's a prescription bottle in my bag, full of Lexapro tablets. I don't take them, I just like to have them with me. Like a security blanket. I put a handful in the almost empty Baggie and put it on the toilet lid, where I grind my heel into it.

"There. They'll never know the difference"

"What'll that do to them?" Kat squints at it.

"Oh, Kat, your concern is heartwarming."

"Well, I don't need two fucking dead Penn students on my conscience."

"It'll make them incredibly nauseous and, if it's not the case already, incapable of getting an erection for a couple weeks."

Kat's cackling laughter rings off the cracked tile and plaster. "Awesome. Let's finish these beers, ditch the dorks, and go somewhere better."

"700 Club?"

"Fuck yeah."

When we get back to the booth, I down the end of my beer and grab my bag off the bench.

"I'm gonna go down the street and buy some more cigarettes." I zip my hoodie up. This is my favorite part. "Anyone need anything?" I'm careful not to look Kat in the eye for fear of laughing and blowing our cover.

Bro shakes his head no, and Dude actually shoots me the wink and the gun. I stop for a moment to contemplate the satisfying crunch his knuckle would make if I bent it the wrong way.

Outside, I walk down the street and turn left. I stand outside the corner store and smoke a cigarette. I scrounge some change from the bottom of my bag and call Kat's cell from a porno-papered pay phone outside the store. It rings twice.

"Hello?"

"Alright, let's ditch these fuckers. I'm bored."

"Oh shit, yeah. Your wallet's right here. Yeah. On the table. I'll run it down to you."

"And the Oscar goes to . . ." I smirk and hang up. The familiar rush of blood hits my ears. I become aware of my heartbeat. I breathe in deep, letting the high hit me. My skin tingles.

We're walking north on Fifteenth surrounded by throngs of after-work drinkers. Thick postgrads in shirts and ties. Middle-aged administrators in high-waisted, well-creased slacks.

"You know, we don't have any money for a cab, and 700 Club's all the way up in Northern Liberties."

"So we hoof it. What? Forty-five minutes?" My

steps are lighter. I'm spurred on by my old friend, amphetamine. Could walk anywhere.

"I'm up for that. Besides, it'd be an embarrassment to show up before ten."

"Yes, we mustn't forget our hipster code of conduct."

"You know hipster boys are way less likely to buy us drinks."

"That's 'cause our hair's all one length. And who cares anyway? I'm high as a kite for now, and at least it'll be so loud in there I won't have to listen to anyone speak."

The club used to be a town house. Downstairs is a long, narrow bar. Upstairs is a smaller bar, a dance floor, and a room full of armchairs and couches. When we get there it's pretty packed for a Monday. We push into the throng of shaggy heads and skinny jeans. We bypass the downstairs bar since we are dead broke and head up the stairs to the dance floor.

The DJ's playing the Buzzcocks' "What Do I Get?" This is a good sign.

Kat nudges me as we top the stairs. She stands on her tiptoes to yell into my ear, over the music.

"We're money, baby."

"Why?"

"See the bartender?" She points into the corner

where the kitchen has been converted into a bar. "I fucked him last weekend. He is so into me."

"Who isn't?"

Kat is giggling with the bartender, tossing her dark curls over her shoulder. I lean my back against the bar and rest my elbows on it. Glancing over my shoulder at her next to me. Does she ever switch off? It's not long before she hands me a bottle of Yuengling.

"On the house." She smirks.

I turn to face the bartender.

"Thanks, man." He's just her type. Long blond dreads and a thick beard.

"No worries. Let me know if you need anything else." He's talking to me but looking at Kat.

I'm half in the bag, desperately attempting to climb all the way in the bag. Kat's off dancing somewhere, and I'm perching on the back of one of the old battered sofas next to the dance floor when this guy sits on the couch below and beside me. He catches my eye and nods. I nod back. My leg is twitching uncontrollably. I put my hand on my knee to stop it.

His hair is dark black, probably a dye job, and he's used an obscene amount of product to get it to look as if he just rolled out of bed. He takes out a pack of Lucky Strikes and lights one. He looks up and catches me watching him. I blurt out an uncomfortable laugh.

"Smoke?" He extends the pack to me.

"Thanks." I never know which end to light on an unfiltered cigarette. Does it matter?

We sit silently for a few minutes, watching the crowd of dancers hump and molest each other. My leg is twitching again.

Eventually Couch Boy hoists himself up onto the back of the couch next to me. Catching my eye, he smiles. I try to smile back, but I'm afraid it looks strained, false. It probably is.

"Hey. I'm Kevin." He extends a hand to me. His right forearm is wrapped in a sleeve of Japanese-style tattoos. Birds and goldfish.

"Hi." I shake his hand but don't offer a name. I haven't come up with a good one yet. Something . . . appropriate for the situation. I finish off the last swig of my beer.

"D'you want another drink?" He points at my empty bottle.

I guess Kat's hypothesis about hipster boys was wrong.

"Yeah, sure. Thanks."

After a few minutes he comes back with my beer and his friend. They're arguing about something. They stand in front of me.

"I don't know about this, man." Couch Boy.

"What? We're not ripping a person off, we're ripping the bar off." His friend's a bit preppy. Popped collar, distressed jeans. Frat boy. "Hey, maybe your friend'll help us." He gestures at me with his beer.

"With what?" I'm curious, and all jacked up.

"Well," Couch Boy starts, "my friend found a credit card in the cab on the way here. He wants to try and open a tab with it at the bar."

"OK . . ."

"See," Frat Boy jumps in enthusiastically, "we open the tab, drink all night, and then just leave the card here. Never close out the tab. The bar can't process the charges without a signature—they'll wait for the person to come back in and collect the card. When no one ever does, if they try to process it, the card will probably have been canceled already. So whoever owns the card won't have to pay for our drinks, the bar will."

"So what's stopping you?"

"The name on the card," Couch Boy again, "is Jessica. We'd need a girl to do it."

I think about it. I assume they're scamming me, but I can't see how. They don't know my name, it's not like they could grass me up. And hell, I'm broke.

"I'm in."

"Awesome!" Frat Boy high-fives me. Oh my god, I just high-fived a stranger. That really must have been good coke. Couch Boy shakes his head a bit, but I can see he's smiling.

I go to the downstairs bar with the boys since they only do cash upstairs, and I want to avoid Kat's bartender in case she told him my real name. I let the bartender know the boys are on my tab so they can use it all night, and we order more beers and some tequila shots.

I'm fucking drunk. What time is it? I lost count of the shots at least an hour ago and Kat even longer before that. Dumb slut's probably screwing the bartender in the basement.

I slam into the railing of the stairs on my way back up to the dance floor and put my hands out in front of me to catch myself on the step above.

"Whoa there."

Couch Boy is behind me; he puts his hand on my back and helps me up.

"I'm fine." I slosh my umpteenth beer onto his arm as I clutch it for support.

"Alright, it's cool."

He's nice. He's being really nice to me. Stop being such a bitch to him. He's cute. I grab the front of his T-shirt.

"You're cute," I slur at him, practically pouring my beer down his front.

"Ha, thanks." He pries my fingers open, releasing himself from my drunken, viselike grip. I gotta chill out. I'll scare him. I lean against the wall behind me and slowly slide down it till I'm sitting on the sticky, ash-covered floor.

"Hey, come on. Let's go sit on the couch." He extends a hand to help me up.

"I got it, I got it," I insist as I try to heave myself back upright, putting my palms into the booze-ash paste on the floor. It's taking me forever to get up, and I nearly take us both down the stairs once I manage it.

We go over to the couch and I sit heavily on it, again spilling my beer. This time on me. He sits next to me.

"Do you want me to call you a cab?"

I start laughing hysterically. I have zero dollars.

"No. No, don't call me a cab. No thanks."

"Right."

He's so nice. Why is he being so nice to me? I put my hand on his knee and try to smile seductively at him, but I'm sure I just look like a leering baboon at this point, having lost all control of my facial muscles.

He removes my hand from his leg, but I refuse to let it go. I put it higher up on his thigh this time.

"Why don't you just take me home with woo. With you." I tap his nose with my index finger. That's cute, right?

"Look, you're pretty drunk. Where's your friend? Maybe you should go home."

"Fuck my friend. And fuck you." After three tries I

manage to hoist myself off the couch. I don't need to sit here and be rejected.

"Hey, hold on . . ."

"Just fuck off." I give him the finger and stumble off toward the bathroom. When I get there, Frat Boy is just coming out.

Fuck it. He'll do.

I grab him by the arm and pull him back into the tiny unisex bathroom.

"Whoa, I like where this is going."

I bet you do. Probably the first time you'll get some without having to date-rape some anorexic sorority sister.

I know I don't really want to be doing this, but it doesn't matter. I push him up against the bathroom door and basically inject my tongue into his mouth. He's a little taken aback, but it doesn't take him long to realize what's going on. His tongue is halfway down my throat and his hands are halfway down my pants. I don't want him to touch me. I pull his hands out and try to undo his belt. I don't seem to be able to perform this simple task so he takes over. Within seconds his pants are around his ankles.

"Sit down." I push him onto the toilet lid. I kneel on the tile and feel the piss-beer water start to soak through my jeans. It doesn't matter. I take out his cock and it's only a half-stack. Should I be offended?

I suck him hard.

What the fuck is the point of this? I'm sucking off some asshole frat boy in this filthy bathroom for absolutely no reason.

I start to feel sick and try to stop, but I feel a hand on my head. I push against it but it pushes back harder. I start to choke. Drool is dribbling down his dick. Fuck you, asshole. I should bite down. Grab his balls and twist.

Suddenly, he's got my head with both hands and is thrusting deep into my throat. I gag and a wave of nausea hits me. I push against his stomach with both hands but it's too late. I can feel the warm, snotty glob of cum in the back of my throat.

I swallow.

Then I puke.

All over the dickhead's cock and boxers and thighs. Serves him right.

"You fucking bitch!" He shoves me away and I lose my balance, sitting down heavily on the wet tile.

I'm laughing. I'm laughing so hard that it hurts. I can't stop.

"You think this is fucking funny, you whore!" He smacks me. Hard. Right across the jaw. I'm too drunk to feel it, and it just makes me laugh harder. He's trying to clean himself off, and I use the sink to pull myself up.

I want to punch him. But I don't know if I can. I'm afraid of what he'll do if I try. I unlatch the door and stumble back out into the bar.

I can't tell if I'm still laughing or if I'm crying now. It doesn't matter.

What would The Stranger think if he could see me now? What kind of person would he think I was?

What kind of person am I?

I wake up sweating.

Fuck, my head is killing me.

I have no clue where the hell I am, or how I got here.

I sit up, pulling a ratty crocheted throw off me. There's thick sunlight trying to push its way through heavy green curtains. I'm on a rough couch in a dingy living room.

Chipmunk's living room.

Thank god.

Kat must have brought me here as it's her usual crash pad. She doesn't live here. She doesn't live anywhere. And Chipmunk's a total pushover.

Right, what do I remember?

Credit card fraud, that was fun . . . and Couch Boy, ooh, I think I gave him the finger . . . oh shit . . . asshole-frat-boy-friend-of-couch-boy . . . and the bathroom.

I am a fucking idiot.

A now familiar wave of nausea hits me and I leg it through the dining room and into the kitchen. I manage to get most of my puke in the sink. It's thin and watery and tastes like tequila. Well, and puke. Some of it sloshes around in someone's milky cereal bowl. I run the water to rinse it down the drain.

My head is throbbing and my hairline and upper lip are wet. I get a glass of water and head back to the couch.

I don't remember anything after the bathroom. I wish I didn't remember anything before the bathroom. Well, I wish I didn't remember the bathroom.

I touch the side of my face and it's sore. My lip hurts, too. I brush it lightly and flakes of dry blood come away on my fingertips.

Asshole split my lip.

There are footsteps on the stairs.

Kat comes in wearing a yellow tank top and pink underwear.

"I heard you retching. Did you boot?"

"Yeah. In the sink."

"Ha, loser."

"Yeah, fuck off. What happened last night? How'd I get here?"

"That guy, with the hair, he found me. Asked if I'd take you home. He called us a cab. Paid for it, too."

"What guy? Not the frat boy?"

"No, no, the hipster, with the hair."

"Really?" I fucked up, bad style.

"Yeah, I think he *liiiikes* you." She drags the word out in that schoolyard way. "Did you get digits?"

"No."

"Why not?"

"I don't know. Too drunk."

What's the point? What's the point of getting a number, or of anyone being into me? I'm just a dumb, drunk slut. Crazy and insecure. Toward the end there, Daniel and I were always drunk. We couldn't even look each other in the face when we were sober. And when we were drunk we just fought.

The night I found that note from Jamie in his wallet. All his friends were at our house. Drinking, singing, having a good time. And that fucking note. She'd written it to him right after we'd gotten together. Something about how disappointed she was that he'd found someone else. About how she always thought they'd get back together . . . get married even. Fucking bitch dumped him. Cheated on him even. I was so mad that he'd kept it. That he kept it close to him, in his wallet. I flipped out, screamed at him in front of all the boys. We nearly broke up that night.

Guess he's a sucker for dumb sluts.

He didn't deserve it. Didn't deserve me.

I just figured someone who could love me had to be more fucked up than I was.

How the fuck did he put up with it for so long?

Why? Was it worth it for him? Worth getting his heart broken in the end? My being able to break his heart negates any sense of cosmic justice.

He should have been allowed to break mine.

Kat's voice severs my thoughts. ". . . and so Ben's mad at me . . . I think . . . Hello? Asshole, are you listening?"

"Were you talking?"

Walking west on Pine the air smells of cigarettes and greasy pizza. I pass an old man walking a golden retriever. I smile a little. I always smile at dogs and not the people walking them.

My hand trembles as I try to unlock the front door to my building. It's just an old town house. There's one other studio on the third floor with mine, and the landlord's office is the only thing on the second floor.

I see someone walking down the street toward me in a long, dark coat, and for a moment I think it's him. But I know that even in this town that kind of coincidence is slightly out of the ordinary.

As he gets closer my heart slips into my intestines.

It *is* him. Again. Like some kind of dark guardian angel who only appears when there's no one around to see him. The Stranger.

My Stranger.

This has to be some kind of sign. Do I believe in signs?

Today I do.

As he walks toward me he lifts his eyes and they meet mine. Everything slows, like in a bad romantic comedy. Close-up on his lashes lifting. Cue "I Think I See the Light" by Cat Stevens. Camera pulls out as we make eye contact.

Recognition.

He smiles, broadly. In painful slow motion, his teeth are revealed, two by two. He tips his head to me, hair swooping grandly into his face.

In the movie, I smile slyly, looking up from under my lashes. Maybe send a ripple of fingers toward him.

In reality, my lips press a tight half-smile and I drop my keys. *Music screeches to a halt.*

He continues past and I flash back to the night before. Could he read the disgrace on my face? Do I look and smell like someone who let themselves get face-fucked in a dingy bar bathroom? Is he disgusted by me, but isn't sure why?

I follow the back of his dark head up Eleventh Street until it turns a corner.

Fuckfuckfuck. Why didn't I say anything? I could have been charming. I'm sure I've been charming before.

And now he knows where I live. It would be too much to hope that he's been trying to find out. I want to know where he lives. If he has a wife, kids. If he's happy.

If he could make me happy.

He turns left on Lombard, away from the subway. He doesn't live in Jersey. He lives somewhere near here. Right around the corner.

If I follow him, we'll be even.

I jog up the block, afraid of losing him but also afraid of coming face-to-face with him. As I turn onto Lombard I see him at the opposite end of the block, climbing the stoop to the corner town house.

No fucking shit. He does live around the corner.

I must have passed him before. What was different on the train? Is the shared appreciation of a good book and one masturbatory fantasy enough to base a crush on?

I duck into the park across the street and find a bench where I can make him out, then light a cigarette. It's less a park and more just a square of freshly laid brick enclosed by young trees. Man-made greenspace, included on the block in a vain attempt to counterbalance the cold stoniness of the city.

Leaning back, I try to look inconspicuous, but I can't help crossing and recrossing my legs. My foot flaps nervously. I draw too intensely on my cigarette, and it makes my head swim. I have to shut my eyes and take a lungful of gritty city air.

I watch from the side of my eyes as he unlocks his heavy blue front door and goes inside. Once it's closed behind him I allow my head to right itself, looking directly at the house's redbrick front.

It's a single home. Somehow it's managed to avoid being chopped, gutted, and segmented into separate apartments.

It has maintained its completeness.

The street is narrow, and so his house is close enough to give me an unobstructed view into his living room through a large bay window. Navy curtains are parted to reveal a simple, comfortable room. The colors are masculine, the wood, dark. He crosses through his living room and into what I assume is the kitchen behind it. A small rectangle of light appears as he flips his switch.

I sit and wait, unmoving, while he's in the kitchen. When he comes back out he's carrying a plate of something. I can't tell what it is, but he reads while he eats it. I can't see a TV. No sign of another person. No sign of a wife.

It occurs to me that he might be gay. We do live in the part of town affectionately referred to as the Gayborhood. He's at least forty, well dressed, and seems to be living alone.

I choose to delude myself, as usual, and tell myself he's straight.

Eventually, he heads upstairs. The light in a room facing me goes on. The curtains are closed, but not completely, and a vertical strip of light bisects the window.

Must be his bedroom. I can see flickers of movement as he passes the opening.

Undressing.

I sit completely still, eyes straining and scrabbling for a sliver of flesh as he bends and moves, walks around the room, discarding clothes. First an elbow, the curve of a back, a flick of dark hair.

I watch. Watch the light in the bathroom go on. Watch his shadowy movements behind the closed blinds. I imagine he's shaving, brushing his teeth. The movements stop but the light stays. He's showering. I can picture him, wet and slick under the showerhead, washing his hair, soaping his face, under his arms, his cock. Does it give him an erection? His slippery soapy hand around his dick? I decide that it does. And that he decides to take it all the way to the end. Pulling gently at first, then harder. Sliding the foreskin I've decided he has, back and forth. Leaning with one hand against the shower wall, head bent under the spray.

Thinking about me.

My stomach is boiling. That familiar ball of anxiety tightens in on itself, begs to be released. Heat rips through my chest. My fingers and mouth tingle with the numbness that comes with lack of oxygen. I know this feeling.

This is how a panic attack starts.

I know I should close my eyes. Drop my head

between my knees, take deep lungfuls of air, but I'm frozen, can't turn my head, flick a finger, blink. I could easily chalk the paralysis up to the attack, but this time I know it's also my unwillingness to miss a moment of him. My breaths are coming short and quick, and darkness is encroaching on the perimeter of my vision.

I don't want to do this here.

I manage to rip my eyes away, squeeze them tight against the light, and lower my head. Willing my breathing to slow, I imagine myself in his bedroom. Draped nonchalantly across the bed, flipping through a paperback. He's telling me about his day, stripping unhesitatingly. My eyes pass over smooth, clear skin. Across broad shoulders, along elegant arms. Over taut but rounded stomach, down trim, solid legs. Every detail presented.

My breathing is reluctant but eventually starts to even out. My heart drops pace. The sweat on my forehead goes cold.

Fine. For now.

I start awake.

I'm still on the park bench, sitting up. There's a crick in my neck.

The sun is setting and a plum-colored haze hangs over rooftops. His house is dark.

Shit, he left and I missed him. Oh God, what if he saw me here, on this bench, chin to chest, sleeping? Like a bum.

I light a cigarette, stand, and stretch. Joints pop and crack all down my body.

I guess it's finally time to go home.

Walking back to my building, I try to remember how long it's been since I was in my apartment. Certainly not since last Wednesday. Not since last Tuesday, when I left for work at the café. A whole week. That must be a new record for me.

Fuck.

I forgot.

Shitshitshitshitshitshitshitshitshit.

The cat.

Thecatthecatthecatthecatthecatthecat.

I'm running. Panting, straining down Eleventh Street.

Thecatthecatthecatthecatthecatthecat.

How long can a cat live without food? Ages, right? Months? Weeks?

Thecatthecatthecatthecatthecatthecat.

What about water? Not long. Days? Please let the toilet seat be up.

Pleasepleasepleasepleasepleasepleaseplease.

I'm at the door, and I can't fucking unlock it because

my hands're shaking so bad that they feel like they'll wrench themselves right off my fucking wrists.

Pleasepleasepleasepleasepleasepleaseplease.

I'm leaping the stairs two at a time. My arms and back are sweating. Heart pounding in my ears. Stomach eating itself.

I can't hear anything. No pitiful, pleading mewing. But he always cries when he hears me come home. Always, no exceptions.

I can't see to unlock the door to my apartment because hot tears are searing my eyes and cheeks.

"Sal?" I'm whimpering.

Nothing.

"Sali? Salinger?" My key is scraping the lock, desperately looking for the keyhole.

Finally, I'm in. I have to push against crinkling bags of trash, stacked up behind the door.

He doesn't come running.

I scan the one room that is my bedroom/living room/kitchen for his plump gray body. A twitching whisker, a flicking tail. Nothing.

Choking back snot, I approach the bathroom. My heart is sinking lower and lower.

Pleasepleasepleasepleasepleasepleaseplease.

Behind the half-open door, I can see it. The end of a thin, pathetic little tail. Gray and black.

It's still.

I slowly push the door open and there he is. Poor, wretched body stretched out in front of the mortally closed toilet. I can see his little ribs through sagging skin. Big, yellow eyes, clouded and sunken in, to match his cheeks. Mouth, swollen and crusted over. Fat, split little tongue parting cracked lips. Black flakes of blood stick to his nostrils and whiskers. A puddle of vomit has dried in front of him, and a puddle of watery shit has done the same behind him.

What.

Have.

I.

Done?

I walk slowly backward, closing the bathroom door behind me. I stumble over clothes, books, trash, and various apartment debris before sitting heavily on the edge of my unmade bed.

I'm not crying anymore. I'm too shocked. Too appalled at what a self-absorbed little cunt I've become. Appalled at what I am capable of.

It begins again.

The tight anxious grip on my organs. The quickened breath, the tingling. Rush of heat. Rush of fear.

I roll onto my side and pull my knees into my stomach. This time I let the panic take me. I'm not strong enough to battle it. I don't care enough.

I clench my eyes to the overhead light. It's piercing

my brain through my lids, and I'd get up and turn it off if I wasn't completely paralyzed. Paralyzed by fear, by apathy about ever moving again.

The only part of me that moves is my heaving, painful lungs.

I will myself to twitch a finger, a toe, raise an eyebrow, but my body refuses. It doesn't want to move or respond.

Doesn't want to be alive anymore.

Will my organs give up the will to function? What do my kidneys care about filtering my blood? My intestines about making shit? My eyes about seeing? My lungs about breathing?

My heart about beating?

What does my body care if it lives or dies? What do I?

I'm going to die. Here on this bed because my body doesn't think it deserves to live anymore. There's nothing I can do. I'm going to die.

I lay like that for hours. I barely notice when my breathing eventually slows, my heart maintains, my eyes relax. I'm still paralyzed. Incapable of finding the will to move.

Daniel and I were trying desperately to make living together work. He wanted kittens, wanted to pay for it all. His gift to me. They were identical little balls of insubstantial gray fluff when we released them from their plastic cage at the SPCA. Brothers, they told us. Hadn't wanted to split them up. We found out later that Fitz was a girl. We'd named them Salinger and Fitzgerald. Sal and Fitz. Daniel's literary first love was *The Great Gatsby*. And I couldn't stand it. I was always a *Catcher in the Rye* girl myself.

They'd slept at the foot of our bed and licked our eyelids in the morning.

When we split, we split them, too. Like unfortunate children of a gruesome divorce. Fitz off to Daniel's parents' house, where she had lots of room and grass and another cat for her to harass.

And Sal. Poor Salinger. Off to a filthy studio apartment. Left there for days, alone. His attention-craving heart tense with anticipation. Left there for a week, to dry out, choking.

If Daniel knew. Oh, if Daniel knew what I've done. I can see his already cracked heart, disintegrating. A pile of chalky, purple paste. His pale green eyes boring holes into my skull, willing my brain to burst into flames.

I will my brain to burst into flames.

And My Stranger. Someone who could do this. He couldn't love someone who could do this. How can I become someone who wouldn't have done this? I wish he were here. Curled around me, his dark coat still on.

I sob into my pillow, feel the wet warmth spread against my face.

He'd pet me and whisper, "Shh." He'd tell me, "It's OK. It's not your fault. You aren't this person."

I shut my eyes and try to conjure the pressure of his arm tightly encircling my waist. His breath on the back of my neck as he repeats, "You are not this person. You are not this person. You are not this person."

You are not the kind of person who wasted their youth sucking dicks in bathrooms and basements. You are not the kind of person who couldn't love the people who have loved you because you were too busy thinking about yourself. You are not the kind of person who takes responsibility for a soft and innocent life and then lets it die panicking.

I used to be a child. A sweet and smart and shy child. I used to hug my mother every night and tell her I loved her. I used to care about things and get straight As and sing in the school choir.

And too young, and too early, my brain gave up on me. My psyche turned against me. Did all it could to harden my heart and teach me how to hate myself and everything around me. I am my own worst enemy. Because I live in a world where my vote doesn't count? Because everything I do is futile and useless? Because early promise never lives up to its potential? Was this who I was always meant to be?

I am not this person. If I meet him, he won't already know me. I can be whoever I want when I stand before him. I can be better. I can be more. I can be the me I used to be. The me I want to be.

I need him. I'll do whatever it takes.

I wake up with my eyes crusted shut and snot dried to my nostrils. I chip away at my eyelashes with my fingernails, pry them apart. It's the middle of the night. I am surprisingly clearheaded. I know what I need to do. I need to take stock. Then I need to find a way in. A way in to him.

And out of this fucking cage.

The apartment. The apartment is a disaster area. Every available surface, including the floor and the bed, is littered with my scattered life. Garbage, cat hair, filth. It smells like piss and shit. There's a pile of cigarette butts under the corner of my pillow, piles of cat shit under the desk. Dishes are heaped in and around the sink, covered in dried smears of food, scraped in places where the cat had desperately tried to derive some sustenance. It's the apartment of a person who is so emotionally devoid, so corrupt . . . I glance at the bathroom door.

I feel the sting of fresh tears but I inhale sharply, hold it, squeeze my eyes. I refuse to think about it. That wasn't me. That wasn't me who did that.

It was somebody else.

First, I'm going to deal with this apartment. Then I'm going to find out his name.

Somehow.

I plug my phone in and turn it on. Eight messages. A few from Kat, one from Jason, Mom, Chipmunk. I erase them all without listening to them. The last one's from Dad. I listen to that one.

"Hey Baby, it's your Dad. Just checking in on you. Wanna see how you're doing. Hope you're happy and all that. Gimme a call sometime, OK? Alright, I love you, baby. Call me."

I delete that one too.

Happy? Ha.

I haven't spoken to Dad in a while. After a few months and fewer messages the guilt starts to creep in. I think about calling him. But I don't think I can make it sound as if everything's alright. And I learned at a young age that there's no point in telling someone your problems over the phone when they're thousands of miles away. All he can do for me is worry. And I don't like thinking of him feeling that way.

In the back of my closet there's a plastic bucket of cleaning supplies that Mom optimistically bought for me when I first moved in. Most of them have never been opened.

I collect bags and bags of garbage and haul them three at a time down two flights of stairs and pile them on the curb. I collect the stack of mail waiting for me. Bills and junk. I throw it all out without opening it. I fill my laundry basket with clothes covered in ash and cat hair. I stack all the dirty dishes into boxes and take them all out to the curb as well.

I don't go in the bathroom. The door stays closed.

I'm never going in there again.

I scrub and wipe and dust and vacuum and straighten and mop and sweat.

And flash forward.

We're not in his house, we're in our house. We're not in Philadelphia, we're in an undisclosed, perpetually sunny location. I'm on the balcony smoking a cigarette. Hair piled lazily on top of my head. He's inside at his desk, working.

On what, I haven't decided yet.

I stab my cigarette out and come inside. I bend and wrap my arms around his shoulders and across his chest. Burying my nose in his thick hair, I smell him. Heat and smoke and skin. He rests a hand on my wrist, squeezes it, pressing the bones together. I kiss the back of his neck, sweeping his hair aside with my knuckles.

"Coffee?" I bite his earlobe.

"Mmm. Yes." He runs a hand around the back of my neck, pulls me in over his shoulder, twists to kiss me.

As I turn to go he swivels in his chair and smacks my ass.

And I flash backward.

Daniel and I lived in squalor. We had a whole house to ourselves. So cheap because the neighborhood was so bad. Right smack in the middle of North Philly. One day in the summer we heard shots outside. We ran to the bedroom window and watched some really young black guy fire a shot on another young black guy. No one got hurt. For whatever reason, they just dispersed.

It was broad daylight.

We didn't call the cops. No one else did, either. What would have been the point?

The living room was constantly covered in newspapers, fast-food wrappers, pizza boxes, beer bottles. The bedroom was buried in clothes, books. There was a spare room, empty except for a desk, a dartboard, and piles and piles of my school papers, yellowed with dusty sunlight. The kitchen was muddy, the corners filled with leaves that had blown in under the back door. There were dishes in the sink then, too.

We ate takeout every night. Chinese, pizza, buffalo wings. We sat in the living room and watched TV. Cable, courtesy of my mother. We got fat and boring. Bored with life and, subsequently, with each other. It was always the same. I went to class, he went to work. We got drunk. Drink, eat, sleep, rent movies, fuck . . . barely. Slowly, we managed to pull each other deeper and deeper into these comfortable little holes we had unconsciously dug for ourselves. We just crouched there, day after endless day, in the dark. Isolating ourselves from the world, and each other.

It takes hours to clean the apartment, and when I'm finally finished, soft light seeps through my windows. In the distance, I can see the jagged, mirrored peaks of Liberty One and Two tearing like claws into the soft, gray flesh of the sky.

I have a mission now. It's him. I don't know how I know. I just do. I can just tell.

I brush my hair and tie it back. I wash my face with dish soap in the kitchen sink so as to avoid the bathroom and what lurks inside. I can feel the skin pull tight across my skull as it dries. There are a few clean pairs of underwear and a T-shirt or two left from the last time I did laundry at Mom's. I put on one of each, and my dirty jeans again. I roll deodorant under my arms. I don't bother with my teeth.

In the Wawa I get a cup of coffee, a bottle of water, a pack of Marlboro Reds, and a new toothbrush and some toothpaste to keep in the kitchen. I charge it all.

My copy of *A Handful of Dust* is in the bottom of my bag.

I'm camping out.

I settle myself on my bench in the park across from

his house. It's about seven. I flip through the paperback. My eye glancing over underlined phrases, rereading old notes. Things I'd thought and felt years ago. I remember when books could touch me. Bring out some raw emotion that had been lurking inside, nameless. I can't remember the last time I read a book.

I turn pages. I'm looking for something.

I want to see him. Just a flicker of him. I'm afraid I may have made him up. What if, while I'm sitting here, an Asian family comes down for breakfast? A retired couple? What if he doesn't exist? I don't trust my perceptions. Don't trust my brain. I can feel its grip slipping.

Why bother trying to stop it?

I've finished my coffee and two cigarettes by the time his bedroom light goes on. It's just past eight. In the misty light of early day, all I can make out of him are a few fluttering shadows, and the bathroom light going on and off. Finally, he comes downstairs, through the living room and into the kitchen. He's in dark gray pants, a blue collared shirt. No tie.

He walks with purpose, so natural. If he knew I was watching, would he walk differently?

He brings in his mail and his paper, makes himself breakfast, and afterward takes the time to smoke a cigarette while he glances over the headlines. Once he brings his dishes into the kitchen I start to gather my things.

We're going to work.

I follow him deeper into the heart of the city. It stinks of deep fryers, buses, things decomposing. I try to keep him two blocks ahead but have to jog to catch up when he turns corners so I won't lose him. The jungle of twisted metal and scattered cement thickens with each block. Red, yellow, green streetlights blooming and dying on every corner. The dull eyes of the local wild-life. Pressed and polished professionals, mint green medical students, and spiky, inked hipsters.

I dodge between them.

When he finally enters an anonymous office block on Chestnut I slip into a café across the street to nurse a cup of coffee.

What does he do up there?

Most of these buildings are made up of small, inde-pendent offices that anyone can rent. Lawyers, dentists, publishers. Who knows what else? Internet porn entre-preneurs, bookies, dominatrixes.

Dominatrices?

I flip through Waugh some more. I'm looking for something, something I know I underlined. What was it?

I keep one eye on the door he entered.

At 10:45 the bar calls. I assume it's Aidan calling to find out why I haven't shown up for work yet. I let it go to voice mail, then erase the message without listening to it. I have more important things to do right now than sit in that dank, dark, hole of a place and listen to the Walking Irish Hard-On spout shit.

I'm leaving that all behind.

I sit and read, facing the window, but I don't get very far because every three words I glance back across the street, afraid he'll sneak out for lunch without my noticing. Eventually, I admit defeat and put the book facedown on my table and light a cigarette. The snotty baristas are eyeing me coldly, since I've been sitting at this table for an hour and a half and haven't bought anything since my first cup of coffee. But they can fuck off for all I care.

What is it? How do you just know sometimes that someone's going to be important in your life? As soon as you see them? He and I—cliché alert—we're meant to be.

He exists for me.

Daniel used to joke that ten years after we broke up, we'd run into each other somewhere, go for a coffee. I'd tell him all about this great guy I was seeing at the time. How smart, sweet, caring he was. And Daniel would ask me, like in a bad movie, "But does he make you laugh?"

Will he? Will My Stranger make me laugh? In ten years' time, when I'm better and we're together and I do run into Daniel on the street and we do go for coffee and he does ask me that question—in an ironic "remember when I said I'd ask you that?" kind of way—what will my answer be?

I imagine he will. I imagine the first night we meet. When I'm finally ready to sidle up next to him at a bar, flash him a sideways glance. Catch and keep his eye, watch him recognize me, smile. Introduce myself, let him buy me a drink. I imagine we won't be able to stop laughing. Our sense of humor will be the same. We'll talk easily, honestly.

He has to feel that, too.

He must know that I'm here. Here just for him.

I won't fuck it up this time.

A little after one he finally emerges from the office building. A shadowed moth from a concrete cocoon. I hastily shove my things in my bag and have to restrain myself from pressing my clammy face on the glass as I strain to watch him as he heads west.

Once he's just out of my sight line I slide out of the café and head in the same direction. I can see him farther along, on the opposite side of the street. He blinks in and out of view behind the bobbing heads of suited stiffs desperately clamoring in and out of shops, banks, restaurants. Sad little ants in a jumbled heap. Some boring order overarching their apparent chaos.

He's better than that. More than.

At the corner of Walnut and Eighteenth he enters Rittenhouse Square. The Indian summer is pressing on, and sunlight trickles through the trees, spattering like paint on the gray pavement and sickly grass. I walk the perimeter of the park as he cuts diagonally into the heart of it. I keep my eyes trained on him. I nearly run over an older woman wearing too much red lipstick, walking two shih tzus.

He chooses a shaded bench near the center fountain and removes an apple from his black briefcase. I enter the park from a different angle and seat myself on a bench in the neighboring spoke. My back to his. If I sit sideways on the bench, with my feet up, I can twist to see the back of his head about twenty feet away. I light a cigarette and try to remember the last time I had something to eat. I should now, but I can't. My stomach is clawing at my rib cage, trying to pull itself up, climb hand over hand up my throat and out my mouth to lie on the grass, gasping and drying out in the high sun. It doesn't want food. It wants completion. It, with the rest of my body—organs, blood, bones—wants to feel finished, whole. Each cell individually pulls toward him, straining like chained dogs. Threatening at any moment to break free and scatter. Every particle of me separating and kicking off into the smoky, nearly October breeze.

I nearly leap out of my skin when my phone rings. Digging it out of my pocket, I see his head twitch, cocking an ear behind him to catch the incessant bleeping.

It's Jason.

"Hey." I try to keep my voice low, allowing the whirring traffic circling the park to muffle me.

"Hey. I just wanted to see how you're doing. I know you were a bit off this weekend."

"Oh yeah. No, I'm fine now actually. Feeling much better."

"Really? Why? What happened?"

"Well, nothing really. I mean, I met someone."

"That was fast."

"Well, I haven't really met him per se. . . . It's complicated. But it's alright. Everything's gonna be good."

"Are you sure you're alright? You sound . . . I don't know, different."

"I just told you, I'm great."

"So, who is this guy?"

"Look, like I said, it's complicated. I can't really talk about it right now." I could explain it to him. Explain to him how I just know, how this is something I have to do, have to see through to the end. Jason would understand.

But not here. Not yet.

"Are you sure you're OK? Maybe you should give your mom a ring."

"Jay, really, let it go. I have to go. I'll talk to you later." I hang up on him. I'll explain it all in the end, when it's sorted.

When evening comes I follow him back home from work. No happy-hour drinks or dinner dates. I perch on what I now think of as "my bench" and keep watch over his uneventful night at home as the city sky turns from yellow to orange to dark brown. After he eats he heads upstairs and disappears to the back of the house for hours. Finally, when the sky is as dark as it gets around here, and the stars would be out if the city didn't exist, he readies himself for bed and then spends an hour or so reading before he turns off his bedside lamp and goes to sleep.

I leave him to it and head home to do similarly.

At home, I brush my teeth in the kitchen to avoid the bathroom. I can piss in bars till the end of time, but eventually I'll have to find somewhere to take a shower. I'll go to Chipmunk's tomorrow.

Sitting in bed, I put *Beautiful Freak* in my CD player and roll a joint. I lean against my pillows and take in my freshly cleaned studio.

God, I can't fucking wait to move out of here. Move into someplace more fitting a well-adjusted adult. Into a place suitable for beginning a mature relationship. Somewhere out of this city. Far, far away.

My Stranger and me, somewhere new. Somewhere fresh.

When Daniel and I moved in together, we were playing house. What an amateur mistake. We spent money we didn't have furnishing rooms we'd never use. Pretending to be grown-ups. Pretending to start a life together.

When really it was the beginning of the end.

I go to sleep early, as I have a busy day tomorrow. I lie in the dark, picturing the soft expression on My Stranger's face, his hands and mouth as he lights a cigarette, hoping to dream about him. Hoping for the rare but ever-coveted good dream.

In the morning I call Chipmunk.

"My hot water's busted. Can I take a shower at yours?"

"Yeah, sure."

"Be round in an hour."

After watching to be sure My Stranger went in to work, I head to Chimpunk's in South Philly, where town houses become row homes. Thinner, as if they've been squeezed together. Without any yards, people spill out of houses and litter their stoops and sidewalks. Groups of third-generation Italian boys with greased hair loiter on the steps of corner stores and pizza parlors, in tight wifebeaters and baggy shorts, sharing cigarettes between them. Fat mothers sit in plastic lawn chairs on the sidewalks outside their houses, gossiping as their children run half naked through the streets like packs of wild dogs.

The door to Chipmunk's house is unlocked. In the hallway I am enveloped in a comforting haze of marijuana smoke.

In the living room Kat and Chipmunk are sprawled on the floor, both packing bowls. Chipmunk's greasy-haired, pimple-faced roommate, Kevin, is lolling on the couch with a three-foot bong nestled in his crotch. The TV is on. It looks like *Fear Factor*.

Here lies the world's future. Rest in peace.

"Hey, losers." I flop onto the couch next to Kevin, and he silently passes me the bong without breaking gaze from the box.

Kat looks over her shoulder as I take a hit. "Hey, slut."

"Are you seriously watching *Fear Factor*?" I exhale smoke as I speak.

"Hell yes. You missed the maggot milkshakes."

"I'm honestly upset about that."

On the screen they are stringing up a contestant by her ankles over a giant tank of water, which she is gradually lowered into. She takes a lungful of air, puffing out her cheeks. A graphic in the corner starts marking time once her head is submerged.

"Wait . . ." Chipmunk's voice is high-pitched and whiny. The word has two syllables in her mouth. "Way-ayt . . . How do they know they're not breathing?"

Chipmunk is the dumbest person I know.

Kat turns on her.

"Chipmunk, what the fuck are you talking about?"

"How do they know they're not breathing?" She emphasizes the question as if Kat is the one missing something.

"I don't even understand what you're asking. That's how dumb that question is." Kevin and I laugh.

"Wait guys . . . stop. How do they know? Would there be bubbles?" Her pitch peaks excruciatingly on the word *bubbles*.

"Because," I interject, "people don't have gills, asshole."

Chipmunk sits up and turns around to face me. Short blond hair bobbing around her sharp face. She pushes her wire rims up the bridge of her nose.

"What?"

"Because people can't breathe underwater, sweetheart." I pat her condescendingly on the head.

"What? Oh . . . that's not what I meant."

"Whatever, I'm getting in the shower."

When I come back downstairs all the smoking devices have been emptied and repacked. Three pairs of pink bleary eyes stare glassily at the screen, which is now showing *America's Next Top Model.*

"Stay," Kat commands me without tearing her eyes away from the babysitter. "It's a marathon."

"Tempting, but I'll pass." I've got something to do.

Back in my park, on my bench, I take in his house.

His house isn't really the corner. It's the corner house, but there's a narrow alley separating it from the Laundromat that actually occupies the corner plot.

I take a quick glance around me before striding across the street.

Look purposeful. Like you're supposed to be here.

Rationally, I know that breaking into someone's house isn't usually the best way to get to know them. But I haven't been able to find out what he does, who his friends are, what he thinks . . . what he's like, just from following him. I can't tap his phones, intercept his mail, hear his thoughts, or god forbid, approach him in the street in broad daylight and say, 'Hey, let's get to know each other.' I really don't know what else to do.

And to be honest, I just really want to muck about in his stuff.

I bypass his front door because I know he locks it and head down the side alley. There's one window along this wall, at the back, presumably over the kitchen sink. It's high. And thin. The wall below is brick face. No footholds.

At the back of his house is a small patch of yard. Separating it from the alley is a six-foot chain-link fence.

Scalable.

I reach up, grasping metal with both hands. I wedge a toe into the fence and hoist myself up. The chain-link is rusting, worn. It cuts into the creases in my fingers, smearing them with ruddy slashes. I wedge in the other toe and hoist myself up again. By the time I get to the top, I'm panting. The muscles in my arms wobble. I throw a leg over the top, and as I attempt to turn around on the other side, I slip. My arm catches on the top of the fence, and it tears into my skin as I fall. I land on my back in the grass, thumping my head on the packed dirt. I've knocked the wind out of myself, and for whole seconds I can't take a breath. The panic starts to creep in, the fear of death. But suddenly I'm gasping. Choking on the sudden rush of air as my lungs kick back in.

I lie on my back, taking long, slow breaths. Blood pulses in my ears as heat and pain spread like creeping fingers across my scalp. I hold my arm up in front of my face. There's a gash in the skin inches long. Blood runs from it, pooling and splitting at the crease of my elbow.

I run my tongue along the split flesh.

Is that taste me? Can you know yourself by taste? Does all blood have that dirty-penny taste? Or is it just mine? Does someone else's blood taste like milk? Honey? Charcoal?

I lick it again.

I wouldn't want it to smear on anything. The last thing I want is to to leave bloody fingerprints all over his house. Even though I'm breaking in, I don't want to scare the shit out of the guy.

Since there is no access to the street from his back-yard, and we live in a relatively safe area of the city, I can only hope he leaves his back door unlocked. I can only hope some wish has been granted me here today.

As the screen door handle gives way with a satisfy-ing little click, my heart jolts slightly, missing a beat. But when the brass doorknob on the wooden door in-side also turns pliantly, clicking its consent, my heart almost stops beating altogether.

I'm in.

Stepping into his darkened kitchen, I close the door gently behind me. I stand for a minute in the dark, trying to come to grips with the fact that I'm actually in. That it was so easy. Now that I'm here, I have no fucking clue what I'm doing.

What am I doing? Collecting information, yes, but what else?

Imposing myself on his space. Leaving traces of my

DNA to mingle with traces of his. Attempting to forge a connection? Or just avoiding what I really should be doing? Which is to say, waiting to bump into him again and then starting a conversation. A normal, everyday, chit-chat kind of conversation. Like a normal everyday person might do.

It will happen. This first. That later.

I find the light switch and turn it on.

The kitchen is small and graying, but clean. No table or chairs. There's a door leading to a basement in the far-right corner and a door into the living room in the far left. I ignore the basement for now.

I'll do it if I have time.

I start with the fridge. Two-percent milk, block of cheddar cheese. Carton of eggs, with three left. Orange juice. A few tomatoes, a few beers. In the freezer, bag of peas, some pizzas. Pretty banal shit.

The cupboards prove the same. Cereal, pasta, rice . . . things in cans.

I haven't eaten in at least a day and a half and consider making myself a pizza, but my stomach flops in revolt at the thought.

I move to the living room. It's much bigger than it looks from outside, and I was right—no TV. The couches are chocolate brown and overstuffed. I sink into one. Ball myself up in the corner, feet pulled up on the cushions. I shut my eyes and take a sharp breath.

It feels good here. Safe. I can smell it.

I can smell him.

I burrow deeper into the sofa and breathe deep and slow. Letting the tiny molecules of him that are drifting in the air fill my nostrils and my lungs. Feeling them seep through my bronchioli and in to my blood stream. Circulating through my body from my toes to my brain. Through my legs, my stomach, my eyeballs. Through my clit, my uterus, and my heart.

On his coffee table are some scattered newspapers and magazines. A few old issues of *The New Yorker*, the latest *National Geographic*, last Sunday's *New York Times*.

Dull.

Good stuff must be upstairs.

But even his bedroom is frustratingly innocuous. Drawers full of neatly folded T-shirts in dark solid colors. White tube socks, black dress socks, blue boxer shorts. A closet full of collared shirts, white, gray, blue. Dress slacks in black, navy, gray. No suit jackets, no ties. Shoes: a pair of sneakers, sandals and brown dress shoes. He must be wearing his black ones.

The bed neatly made, no clutter.

It's almost unnerving. Where are his *things*?

In the bathroom: razor, toothbrush, toothpaste. The usuals. No weird medicated creams, antipsychotics in little orange bottles, flavored lube.

Nothing.

The man of my dreams cannot be this boring.

There's one more room on this floor, and the door is shut. I open it to find a study. Or an office.

Jackpot.

Up against one wall is a large desk, covered in stacks of papers, folders . . .

Mail.

I dart for the desk, snatching up the first piece of paper I touch. It's a gas bill.

There it is in the top left corner.

C. P. Shorter
1137 Lombard Ave
Philadelphia, PA 19107

His name. I finally know his name. It somehow makes him more real. Like, until now, he may have just been a figment of my lack of imagination. But here it is in black and white. His name.

His identity.

And I find something appealing about the fact that his name is a word.

Shorter. Not the superlative. That would be "shortest." The most short.

No. It's the comparative. More short.

I like that.

You can't expect anyone to be the most. But they can be more.

I can be more.

The C. P. is frustrating. A great mystery only half solved. Maybe he has some horribly effeminate or nerdy name. Like Courtney. Or Cornelius. I can live with that. As long as he has a sense of humor about it. I won't be able to stop myself calling him Corny. Corn-fed. Corn-on-the-cob. Cornholio.

I slip the gas bill into my bag. The bit you fill in is gone, so I can only assume he's paid it.

A spider plant hangs in the one tall window, which fills the wall next to the desk. On the wall behind the desk are two framed photos of the same little girl. She's only about two or three. Her head is covered with thin wisps of coppery hair that shines in that brilliant way only baby hair shines.

A daughter? From a broken marriage? Taken away by an angry mother? Or a treacherous one? Will I be a stepmom before I'm a mom? Can I be?

I can be whatever the fuck I want.

The two walls to my right and left are mostly shelves from the waist up. On these shelves are mostly books.

I start perusing the spines. They're arranged alphabetically by author. I find this appealing. The same way I find those little books of paint sample cards on metal rings appealing.

John Banville, *Book of Evidence*. Javier Marias. A few W. G. Sebald.

I haven't heard of most of them. There are some of my favorites, though. *Midnight's Children*, a few Vonneguts. He must still have the Waugh with him because I can't see it anywhere.

There's no Salinger.

No. Because Salinger is dead.

I stand, shoulders stooped, and begin to sob. Behind my eyelids I can see Sal. Sucked dry. Lifeless on the bathroom floor.

More crying. More dumb, fucking, useless crying.

I sniff hard and straighten.

No more. Get on with it.

I pull *A Handful of Dust* out of my bag and turn to the dog-eared page I finally found. Underlined in blue ink on the top right is one short sentence. "Love is the only thing stronger than sorrow." Stronger. More strong.

I mark the page and slide the book onto his shelf between *Player Piano* and *Trainspotting*. I can only assume this is where he'll try to return his copy, when he's through with it.

I roll out his desk chair and allow myself one good spin before pulling up to his laptop and the pile of both opened and unopened mail. I switch on the laptop, and while it whirs and winks at me, I start opening envelopes.

I am aware that he will undoubtedly know that somebody was here. I'm not trying to hide that fact.

This is a golden opportunity, and I need to take full advantage of it. I can't afford to be tiptoeing around, putting everything back in place.

Might as well make it mean something.

Most of the envelopes contain bills and junk. But there's one, unopened. From J. J. Rothberg & Assoc. I tear into it, scanning the text. "As of September 1, 2005 . . . trial separation . . . proceedings . . . from Jenifer Morley . . . divorce."

I find this oddly heartening.

I leave that one.

I can't find any information regarding what he does for a living. I'll have to Google him.

When Windows boots up I open up his Documents folder. And there it all is. My Photos, My Music, Downloads. And at the bottom, a folder titled "Writings."

I skip the others for now and open this last one.

In the folder is another folder, called "stories."

A writer.

That explains the C. P.

In tiny handwriting on a yellow Post-it, I write, "e. e. cummings, E. M. Forster, H. G. Wells, A. A. Milne, J. M. Barrie, C. D. Rose, T. S. Eliot, C. S. Lewis," I stop myself from thinking J. K. Rowling, "D. H. Lawrence, E. B. White, H. P. Lovecraft," I consider F. Scott then decide against it, "W. H. Auden, V. S. Naipaul, P. G. Wodehouse, W. B. Yeats."

I'm impressed with myself.

At the end I write "C. P. Shorter," and then "J. D. Salinger?" Which I circle. I stick the Post-it on a Sebald.

Sitting back at the computer, I hover the cursor over the "Stories" folder.

Suddenly I'm aware of what a sober moment this is. This could be tragic. If his writing is abhorrent, which is the most likely case, considering most people's writing is abhorrent, than everything I've built up around him, everything I think . . . no, everything I know, is wrong.

But if it's decent, like I know it just has to be, against all odds, then we're in the clear. Good to go.

I open the folder and there are a handful of files. "Nijinsky's Last Jump," "Godfather Death," "On Failing to Get to Lvov."

I read them. I read them all.

And they're beautiful. They really are. They're like fairy tales. Sad and dark and full of magic. Set in dusty far-off places and full of bright colors and thick smells and the tinkle of tiny bells. They wrap around me silkily and sit heavily on me like humid air.

And I really love them.

And thank god, 'cause where might I have turned next if he, my last hope, had failed me?

I get my keys out of my bag and take the pen drive—which my computer dork of a stepfather put in my stocking last Christmas—off its key ring and insert it into the side of his computer. It feels like an intimate act. A coming together. I consider whether I should feel as though I'm violating a boundary of some kind. But decide to trust the fact that I don't.

I save all of his stories onto the stick.

I open his My Photos folder and let my eyes flit over the thumbnails. There aren't many. Some shots of a beach, gray water stretching out to meet a hazy horizon. They all seem to be of places, no people.

There's not enough room for all his music on the stick, so I take the laptop into the bedroom, where I plug it in next to the bed and sit it on a pillow. I open his music and put the whole library on shuffle. I turn the volume up as loud as it will go.

I regret my shower at Chipmunk's because now I am compelled to shower in his shower. Let my nakedness occupy the same space his does every day.

Who says you can't have two showers in a day?

In the bathroom, I leave the door to the bedroom wide open and start getting undressed to an upbeat Latin-sounding song, with lyrics that could be in French. I turn the shower on and run it hot.

I wash my hair with his shampoo; wash my skin with his bar of soap. Shave my legs, armpits, and trim around the edges of my pubes with his disposable razor and shaving cream.

His showerhead is removable, with one of those dials that change the pressure of the spray. Fuck diamonds, a removable pulsating showerhead is a girl's best friend.

I turn it to a strong pulse and put one foot up on the edge of the tub.

I pretend he's here with me, in the shower. His warm, slick chest pressed against my back. I feel his hard cock slip between my wet thighs as he wraps his arms around my waist and pulls me against him. I feel the pressure of his teeth on my shoulder as he twists his hand in my wet hair.

I steadily move the pulsating jet of water on and off my clit. Rocking my hips slowly in rhythm, I lean my forehead on the cool tile and clench my eyes.

He bends me at the waist and I press my palms against the slick porcelain of the wall in front of me to steady myself as he slips himself inside me and groans.

But then it changes. The fantasy becomes me, here, alone, masturbating in his shower. And he comes home, to find me, a stranger, here, dreaming about him. He comes in the bathroom where my back is to him. My eyes are shut. I'm moaning. He creeps up behind me, undoing his belt. Then his shirt. Socks gone, and underwear. I still haven't seen him, I'm too deep in a fantasy about him, to know he's really there. He moves closer and closer to the shower, to me. He stands beside the tub, watching me, touching himself. Then slowly reaches a hand out, and just barely allows his fingertips to brush my naked hip.

I cum.

My fantasy sex life is a thousand times more satisfying than my real sex life.

I could take the word sex out of that thought and it would still be true.

I wrap myself in a plush blue towel and brush my teeth with his toothbrush. I'm convinced that I can taste him, a hint of him, somewhere under the toothpaste.

I haven't really recognized any of the music that's played yet. Some classical piano, latin-y world-type stuff, and one song that I have a sneaking suspicion was the Jesus and Mary Chain.

In his bedroom I dig out one of his clean T-shirts and pull it on. I consider taking one from the dirty laundry but convince myself that that would be a nutcase thing to do. I also adopt a pair of woolly socks before pulling back his comforter and sliding my slick naked legs between his cool sheets.

There are few things in this world that feel as comforting as freshly shaved legs against clean cotton sheets.

I arrange the computer next to me and turn down the volume before letting my wet head sink into his pillows. I roll on my side, pulling the blanket up under my chin and my knees up into my stomach. Closing my eyes, I breathe deep into the pillowcase, trying to learn the smell of him. Of his face and his hair and his breath.

Of his tears and his sweat and his mucus.

Of every molecule of him.

I wake up to an absolutely brilliant song that I've never heard. I lie with my eyes closed and listen to the lyrics. I am drawn to it in a way that I haven't felt with music since high school. It makes me picture the end credits rolling on the film of my life.

In his music player window it says that it's playing "Lazy Line Painter Jane—Belle and Sebastian."

Well, fuck me. That's what I get for talking shit on music I've never actually heard. Score one for the hipsters, I take everything bad I've said about Belle and Sebastian back. And one for Our Mister Shorter for being far hipper in his middle age than I have ever been in my youth.

I smile.

In fact, I feel as though I actually woke up smiling.

It's still light out. The clock on the computer screen says 3:36 but I don't trust it, so I sit up to check the alarm clock. 4:41.

Better get the fuck outta here or I'll be busted.

I keep his T-shirt and socks on but put back on my underwear, jeans, and sneakers. I tuck my socks and T-shirt into my bag. I make the bed as best I can but it's a skill I have always lacked.

Daniel's mom taught me to do hospital corners. When I stayed with them in their rented house in Virginia Beach. It felt stifling. Like she was grooming me to be a good wife. But she was probably just being a good mother. Trying to take care of us. When I tried to do it later I couldn't remember how.

And I did want to be Daniel's wife. But I don't know if I ever thought about how to be a good one.

Instead of leaving through the back door and braving the fence again, I leave through the front door. I lock the handle, but without a key, I can't lock the dead bolt.

As I leave I wonder if he'll call the police when he gets in. It's a definite possibility. Obvious B&E. But what harm did I do? What'd I take? A T-shirt and a gas bill? Even if he does call the cops, it won't exactly be high on their priority list.

I like to think he'll be more intrigued than concerned.

From my perch I watch him return home from work.
I'm surprised by my nervous excitement as I wait for
his reaction to the mild disturbance I've left in his living space.

He doesn't eat but goes directly upstairs to the
bathroom. The light stays on for a while. I left my wet
towel hanging on the back of his bathroom door. Will
he notice?

I pick at a coke scab in my left nostril with the nail
of my pinkie finger as I wait for him to emerge and the
sting of it brings tears to my eyes.

After a bit I can see him moving behind the half-
open curtains in his bedroom. He pulls them to the side
and peers out with a cordless phone pressed to the
side of his head. He glances up and down the street
before pulling the curtains closed entirely.

Who did he call? The police? A friend? Is he scared?
Amused?

He comes downstairs into the living room in boxers
and a T-shirt. The phone is still against his ear, and in
his other hand he is gripping two copies of what I recognize as *A Handful of Dust* . . . and a yellow Post-it.

Has he opened it yet? Seen the message I left him?

He sits heavily on the couch. Tossing the books

onto the coffee table, he runs his hand through his hair and shakes his head. He gestures frantically, brows furrowed, mouth turned down, as he speaks into the receiver. He doesn't look happy.

If only he knew. If only I could walk up to his door, ring the bell. Explain it was me, and throw my arms around him. Sink into him. But I can't yet. I'm not ready.

He sits still, quiet, listening intently to the voice through the line. And then he cracks a smile.

And then he laughs.

I don't know how to feel about this. I want to be relieved that someone has made him see reason about this situation. That this could be a good thing. But there's a sinking feeling as well, that someone somewhere is making him laugh. Making him comfortable in an uncomfortable situation.

Doing my job.

A sharp spark fires in my brain somewhere.

He's chatting calmly now. His body has relaxed into the sofa, and I try desperately to loosen the vise that is tightening around my heart.

Who is it? Who makes him smile that way?

Finally he hangs up and heads back upstairs. With the curtains drawn tight I can only imagine that the brief fluttering shadows I can make out are him dressing. Or better yet, undressing.

But shortly he comes back downstairs in what I can only assume are a fresh shirt and pants, although his wardrobe is so nondescript it's hard to tell.

And then before I realize what's happening, he's thrown on his dark coat and is out the front door. He's going out.

He's going out? Where? With who?

With panic boiling my blood, I follow him west into the heart of the city. It's Friday night, and there are vicious packs of nine-to-fivers crowding the street corners, hanging out of bars, and lounging around sidewalk tables. Talking loudly, flirting, getting drunk. I want to spit on their high heels, choke them with their own neckties. I want them all to shut up and disappear. Leaving him and me alone in the darkened streets to wander arm in arm along the yellow dividing lines.

He stops outside Tria, on the corner of Nineteenth and Walnut. From a block away I can see him smooth the front of his shirt and ruffle his thick hair before climbing the steps into the tiny upscale wine-and-cheese bar.

Once he's inside I approach the entrance. I'm not dressed for this. Not prepared.

The hostess is at least a head shorter than me. Dressed all in black, with black cat-eyed glasses and short-cropped black hair. She reminds me of everyone I've ever seen in McGlinchey's.

Do I just think everyone is a hipster, or has everyone actually become one?

I want to tell her that uneven bangs aren't flattering on anyone, but instead I just ask her if I can sit at the bar.

They don't have any normal beer, just expensive European crap, so I order a pint of the cheapest.

I peer back over my hunched shoulders and see him sitting at a table by the window, alone. But he's waiting for someone, I can tell. He orders a bottle of wine, red. I wonder how expensive it is. Top-shelf? Or second from the bottom?

And then suddenly she's there. And I know it's her the second she walks through the door. Thin, beautiful, blond. Completely put together in a red dress. Everything I'm not. Everything I never wanted to be. Until right now.

He stands to greet her. Kisses the corner of her mouth with a hand on the small of her back. I consider what it would feel like to slit her throat and gut her like a fish. Crack her rib cage and rearrange her organs. Lungs in her skull, heart in her lower intestines, liver jammed into her windpipe. Then sew her back up, bring her back to life, just for moment, to watch her splutter and collapse and die again.

I clench my fists on the bar, digging my jagged

fingernails into my sweaty palms. I'm afraid I'll choke on my own anger before I get a chance to choke *her* with it.

It looks like a first date . . . or at least an early one. I don't really want to be here. I don't want to watch this romance "blossoming." Every flick of her sleek hair, every graze of his fingers on her arm makes me want to jump up on this bar stool and start smashing glasses, screaming obscenities.

Dumb fucking cunt! *Smash.* Fucking bitch slut blond twat! *Smash.* Whore! *Smash.* Ax wound! *Smash.* Slit! *Smash.* Gash! *Smash.* Hole! *Smash.* Snatch!

Smash. Smash. Smash.

But I can't throw things and curse. And I can't leave. I have to know. I have to sit here and take it. Take my fucking punishment.

So I open a tab and decide to get steadily drunk.

Daniel and I went on our first date a few weeks after we had starting seeing each other. We'd been spending afternoons on campus together, evenings at my house or in his dorm. Out in bars with friends. And he wanted the romance. The romance of a "first date." Something that meant something. Something meaningful.

I met him outside the subway stop in Old City. Tight jeans, plunging neckline. Hair washed and brushed.

Mascara even.

Back when I was still trying.

Do I even own any makeup anymore?

He wore gray slacks and a blue dress shirt. His five o'clock shadow neat and trimmed. He was never clean-shaven, not once in the three years I knew him. Said it made his face look fat. I found this piece of vanity endearing.

We walked arm in arm past other young daters, polished and shining in a vaguely pathetic attempt to impress one another.

He turned to me. "Look at them. They've got nothing on us. Everyone's jealous of our youth and beauty." He put us above them. Somehow our fluttering hearts and tingling touches meant more than theirs. And they did, because they were ours.

The Ritz was showing *Metropolis*, a movie we'd connected on during one of our many languorous afternoons, sprawled out on the limited greenspace on Temple's campus, drawing on each other's arms and volleying what we thought was witty banter.

He fell in love with me when I used the word *diagetic* correctly.

We held hands in the theater like hormone-pumping high school sophomores and whispered our appreciation of the really great scenes hotly into each other's ears.

The possibility that My Stranger . . . Mr. Shorter,

as it were, might be feeling that same way about this blond piece of shit makes me want to gut *myself* like a fish. Rip my hot, bleeding heart out of my chest, ram a steak knife into it, pack it in a shoe box, and mail it to her with a note: "Look what you've done to me."

When they get their bill, I pay my tab on the credit card and leave the bar. Head buzzing with thick, foreign lager. I lean against the wall at the corner and light a cigarette. I pray to any god that may be watching me and laughing to please let him walk her home. I have a new mission now, and a cab or a night spent at his house would destroy any hope of fulfilling it.

I have to find a way in.

A way in to *her.*

They exit the bar and cross the street in front of me, her slender pale arm looped through his. I hear in my head the satisfying crack that weak little arm would make if I snapped it across my knee. Like a brittle piece of kindling.

I wait for him to stop on the opposite corner, stretch out his arm, and wave down one of the many yellow taxis hurtling down Walnut Street.

And my breath stops as he does. Or at least he stops and puts his arm out, but car after car speeds past him, backseats packed with passengers. I clench my jaw tight as his arm wavers, slackens, and eventually falls to his side. He turns to her, smiling, says something. The back of her empty blond head nods. They link arms again and continue down Walnut. Away from me. And, I can't help but notice, away from his house.

My jaw relaxes. A god didn't grant me this favor, I know.

A demon did.

It's unnerving how easily I slip into stride a block behind them. I'm becoming too practiced at this act of following. I shouldn't get too used to this. It is only a transition stage, this following, this collecting of information. There is a greater end to these means that I mustn't forget.

Him.

And through him, Me.

The streetlights and headlights and neon bar signs send light from all directions, casting multiple shadows of myself on the pavement around me. One short and black, one stretched and vague. One directly next to me, a darker me painted on storefronts, constantly one step ahead. All the Mes that could exist. All the Mes I could be.

For a moment they all seem more real than the

bone and blood and skin Me that's blocking the light to create them.

All three of us walk for blocks, for what feels like an eternity. He slides an arm around her waist and I cringe. I can feel bits of decayed flesh limply falling from my dying heart.

The city feels tight, looming over me. Imposing a claustrophobic loneliness. I stay as far behind them as I can but know that I could be walking right next to them and they wouldn't notice. I remember what it feels like. When there's only one person in the whole world.

I've tried so hard to be invisible, and now I am.

Be careful what you wish for.

Soon we're in Queen Village, turning down tiny streets with redbrick sidewalks. There are trees here, and the tall, thin town houses shine with modest wealth.

I turn a corner they turned only a minute before and see them climbing the stoop to a house on the other side of the street and down the other end of the block. I quickly turn back around the corner I just came from and peer around the building there, watching their private moment.

She tops the steps, keys in one hand, and his hand in the other. He trails a few steps below, the bridge of their arms spanning the distance between. She turns and leans her back against the door, drawing him up and near. Pulling him close, she rests a hand on his jawline and pulls his mouth to hers.

The kiss is long and deep, and it burns through every inch of me with an excruciating heat. I bow my head and cover my eyes with my hand, pressing hard until little sparks of light and color dance behind my eyelids. Every fantasy flash forward I've had of him and me together comes back to me in an instant, only now instead of me across the table from him, tangled in sheets with him, laughing over drinks with him . . . it's her.

She's invading my future . . . taking over.

I want her gone.

I will her to disappear, to burst into flames, but as I remove my hand from my eyes and open them, there she is with a hand in his hair, his arm around her waist. There she is with her lips pressed against his. There she is, where I should be.

And I hate her. I hate her I hate herIhateherIhateherIhateher.

In the movie, this is where the sky darkens and rain pours down on the protagonist. Me. But the night is warm and dry. The sky indifferent.

What the fuck should it care that my soul is rotting?

Finally, she breaks away, turns her door handle with her back still to it, and enters her house backward, smiling at him. In front of the closed door he stands for a moment, breathing deeply, hands in his pockets. Then he descends the stairs and heads back toward my corner, a heartbreaking spring in his walk.

I contemplate stepping out into sight, waiting on the corner as he approaches, grabbing him by the shoulders and shaking him. What the hell do you think you're doing? You've got it all wrong. You're messing everything up.

But instead I turn and head around the block. Allowing him time to get a good way home ahead of me, and allowing me to swing back around and check her house number.

I want to punish her. I want to slit my wrists in front of her and spray her with my blood. Stain her forever with the pain she's causing me. Make her feel even a fragment of what I feel.

I want to punish her.

Watch out, bitch. You fucked with the wrong person.

I take a meandering route home. Partly to ensure I don't run into him and partly because I need some time to think.

As much as I'd like to, I can't beat the absolute piss out of this woman. I can't confront her at all or let her know who I am in any way. I'd be too culpable. Fingerprints all over his house, then his girlfriend gets the shit kicked out of her. Still, I keep imagining the curbing scene in *American History X,* only it's *her* pearly whites being shattered on the cement and *my* dirty sneaker on the back of her head.

Love has brought out a violent streak in me.

No, I have to scare her. Send her a message. A clear one. Something that'll make her realize he's not worth it. Not worth crossing me.

By the time I unlock my apartment door, I still haven't come up with anything. It has to be perfect. Make karmic sense.

And then, as I open the door and my eyes meet the always-closed bathroom door, it hits me.

Yes. Get my message to the whore and finally eradicate the last remnants of my former self. A cleansing of sorts.

The stench hits me right outside the bathroom door, before I even open it. I take a moment to steel myself for what I know I have to do. This is right. The only way to go.

To end all this.

I crack the door and there's a strange noise. A squishing, living noise. And as I peer inside I realize what it is.

Maggots.

They're squirming. A white roiling mass in poor

little Salinger's gaping mouth and eyes. Coming through a decayed hole in his belly.

I know that all it takes is one rogue fly to make these hundreds of writhing, blind larvae, but I'm always disturbed by how maggots just seem to spring from nowhere. Sudden life, where there wasn't any before. Fresh, ugly life sprouting from death and decay.

I slam the door and retch. Deep dry heaves overtake me and I double over. My eyes sting with heat and tears as my stomach tries to escape my body.

I fall down on my hands and knees, back arching sharply with every shuddering gasp.

I can do this.

I have to do this. Deal with this.

I regain my breath and stand. I'm trembling violently from head to toe. The tears are turning to sobs, but I try to choke them back.

Pull your fucking shit together.

I grab a plastic bag and this time I swing the door wide, breathing through my mouth.

He's not even a cat anymore. Just an empty crumbling shell. What was once fur and skin are now just dead, dry cells. Sloughing off in clumps.

I squat next to him, gritting my teeth. I turn my head away from the scene but have to glance back every once in a while as I put my hands inside the plastic bag and lift his stiff little corpse off the tile floor. I slide my hands out and up the sides of the bag, turning it inside out around him so he and his infestation are now inside it. Like picking up your dog's turd off the sidewalk. A few fat white worms fall from the bag to the floor, where they buck wildly, no longer engulfed in warm, wet flesh and the comforting mass of other fat white worms.

Holding the bag at arm's length, I stand and leave the bathroom. I pick up an old shoe box off my desk and turn it upside down, emptying its contents—old notes, buttons, dried-up pens—onto the floor.

Through the bag, I hold Sal with one hand. I can feel the slight undulation of the bugs through the plastic. With the other hand, I peel the bag back, exposing him just enough to drop him in the shoe box. More maggots tumble onto the carpet and flail.

You deserved better than this, little soul.

Better than me.

I write my note, drop it on top of his not-body, and put the lid on the box.

I wrap it in a brown paper bag and write on the top, "For You." Maybe she'll think it's from him; then she'll definitely open it.

Of course she'll open it. Who wouldn't?

Back outside her house in Queen Village I get the nervous excitement of a child playing Doorbell Dixie. Or like I'm about to set light to a bag of dogshit on my neighbor's porch.

In essence, this is the same game. Dead Cat Dixie.

I set the box on the mat outside her door. I think about saying something to Sal. But this isn't Sal. The thing in this box is just food. Matter. You can only say sorry to a rotting corpse so many times before you just have to let go.

I ready myself, then press hard on her doorbell before sprinting down the stairs and to the end of the street, where I crouch down in my previous spying spot. I don't dare peer around right away. I count to thirty, slowly, chest heaving with even this minor exertion. When I do look, the door is just closing and the box is gone. I count to thirty again, then sixty. I worry for a second that the smell reached her before she could open it, and she's become too suspicious to risk it.

But then it comes.

A high-pitched scream that falls into wailing sobs.

The sound was supposed to be satisfying. This was supposed to be purging. Leaving me clean and ready to truly embrace the new person I will be for him. But the sound cuts me, and haunts me. Floating just behind me as I walk farther and farther from her doorstep.

Who committed this act? A last act from the horrible useless person I was, or the first act of the supposedly better person I am trying to be?

He couldn't love the person who let that cat die, so what makes me think he can love the person who disposed of its corpse this way?

Oh god, what the fuck am I doing?

Nothing makes sense anymore.

I sit on the stoop of a closed café and take a few deep breaths. Visions flash in my head of gaping eye sockets, clumps of hair, and writhing maggots.

Did she really deserve that? Do I really think that was the right thing to do?

I have no answers.

My phone rings and, for the first time in a week, I'm grateful. Any excuse to push this to the back of my head. Any distraction.

It's Kat.

"Thank god." I run my fingers through my hair, and they get caught in the tangles.

"Well, that's an unexpectedly positive greeting."

"Kat, I don't know why you called, but can we please go get drunk?"

"Holy Jesus, you read my mind."

"I'll see you at Tattooed Mom's in ten."

"Done and done."

The bar is cramped and dim. The walls and ceiling are completely collaged with show posters, band flyers, bumper stickers, offensive cartoons, and general bizarre and papery paraphernalia. The long, narrow room is just barely lit by strings of haphazardly hung white Christmas lights. The rough floorboards and the exposed roof rafters are made of the same dark, decaying wood. I slide onto a red leather stool and lean my elbows on the bar, cluttered with tiny plastic bracelets in neon colors, multiflavored Dum-Dums, and various cheap plastic toys.

I press the heels of my palms into my eye sockets, letting my hair fall in front of me.

Luckily it's quiet for a Friday night, and the bartender approaches me almost immediately, munching on waffle fries, which sit on wax paper in a red plastic basket. She is a short black girl. Fairly fat, but black women seem to have the good genetic luck to carry their weight in their tits and asses. She's got a practically flawless weave that cascades around her head and down her chest in slick, tight ringlets. She's wearing gold hoop earrings so big they brush her shoulders, and giant plastic sunglasses even though she's inside this pathetically lit, windowless room in the middle of the night.

I am intensely impressed by her.

I fucking love this place. They have Pabst on draught, and it's only two bucks a pint. I'm riding the last twenty bucks the MAC machine will give me, and I'm determined to get as fucked on that as is humanly possible. I can see relief swimming at the bottom of a pint glass.

The sexy bartender pulls my pint and takes my money, passing back and forth in front of a case of lamp-heated corn dogs. When she brings me my change, I leave a buck on the bar before wandering into the back room. There are a few groups of mismatched people sitting in and among the old bumper cars and roller coaster carts that make up most of the seating. There are a few battered old couches with garishly floral upholstery, discolored and worn from years of spilled drinks, cigarette smoke, and fat asses.

I settle *my* fat ass into the corner of one of these and spark a Marlboro. The walls are almost completely covered with velvet paintings of Michael Jackson, Elvis Presley, and Jesus. All heavily graffitied. "Ass fucking crack pipe smoking pussy," "AIDS SIDS," "I'm Pro-Terror, and I'm a Voter."

Clever little fuckers, aren't they?

I'm almost through my second beer before Kat shows up.

"Hey loser, what the fuck's up with you?"

"I think I did something really stupid tonight."

"Tell me about it, I introduced Ben to Steve last night. Whoa, big mistake."

And instantly we're on Kat. Not a "how're you doing?" Not even a brief glimmer of a thought for the other person.

Which is worse? Someone who is completely self-

absorbed but is oblivious to it or someone who is completely self-absorbed and is constantly tortured by it?
And, in being tortured by it, becomes even more self-
absorbed? And therefore even more tortured . . .

But it's a relief. I just listen to her rattle on, trying
to let myself be distracted from the reality of my situation. Of which I am not entirely sure.

Kat has managed to rope some underage undergrad
into spending all his parents' money on supplying us
with Jäger shots for the last two hours. Not to mention
a handful of PBRs and a pack of Camels. Kid's a fucking gold mine.

And I'm half cut, looking very forward to being
whole cut.

Kat's yammering away and giggling and flirting.
Jailbait McGee is literally just staring at her tits, paying absolutely no attention to anything that's coming
out of her mouth. By the looks of it he's too busy thinking about the things he could stuff in it.

At least that would shut her up.

I am chain-smoking. I am twitchy. And over the
music, faintly, like it's coming from outside and down
the street . . . I think I can hear screaming.

"Hey, asshole." Kat smacks my arm with the backs
of her fingers.

"What?"

"I dare you to go stick a coin in that slot." She points to where two girls are sitting next to each other on bar stools with their backs to us. One girl's jeans are riding so low on her as she hunches over, arms across knees, that there's a good two inches of her fucking ass crack hanging out for all of creation to fucking admire.

"For fuck's sake. I hate that fucking shit," I spit at Kat. "The world is full of fucking useless people. Speaker and present company *not* excluded."

"Tell us how you really feel, sunshine."

"Yeah, well, she deserves a punch in the face." I feel actual hatred for this girl I don't even know. True and honest hate. And I am aware, as usual, that it is not really her that I hate. "I have to piss."

I get up and head toward the bathroom.

And as I pass Coinslot and her friend . . . I don't even really know I'm going to do it. It just happens. I take a drag on my cigarette, take it out of my mouth . . . and stick it, filter end down, in Coinslot's coinslot.

Then just continue past and into the bathroom.

Inside I run my hands under the faucet and splash water on my face. For fuck's sake. What the hell did I do that for? I have to go back out there, where those skanks are gonna kick the living shit out of me.

I piss. Then stare at myself in the mirror.

Fuck it. Let 'em.

Back out in the bar, Skank One and Skank Two are no longer in their seats. I sit back down with Kat.

"Where'd they go?"

Kat turns her attention away from Moneybags and smiles at me.

"Ha, that was awes—"

There's a sharp pain in my scalp as my head jerks back. Someone's got me by the hair.

"Fuck! Shit!" Then a blunt pain across the side of my face as fist hits eye socket. Then another, the mouth, then the nose. I hear Kat.

"Get the fuck off her, you fucking piece of shit cunt!"

I slam onto the floor and lose all my wind as a shoe makes contact and sinks into my stomach.

And then it stops.

I open my eyes to Coinslot being led off by the bartender. She doesn't look happy.

"I'm not done with you, bitch!" She hurls at me on her way out of the bar.

"Fuck you, cunt," I mumble, mostly to myself.

Someone slides hands under my arms and helps me to my feet. I turn, expecting Kat, but it's some guy. Thirties, black hair, nice suit. Too nice for this bar. Probably cruising for trannie prostitutes.

"You alright?" He puts a hand on my back, right over my bra clasp.

"Fuck off." I shrug his hand off and sneer at him over my shoulder as I make my way to the bar. Fuck off. Don't touch me, don't get near me . . . don't get close to me. It's fucking dangerous down here.

Where the fuck is Kat?

Back in the bathroom I give myself a once-over. Split lip . . . again, already swelling up, numbly. Side of my head is throbbing but no sign of a shiner yet. My upper lip is smeared with blood from my nose. There are drops on my T-shirt. I take it off and turn it inside out before putting it back on. I rub water on my mouth. Red splashes into the sink, dispersing almost instantly into the swirling water.

Hands spread on the counter, I press my forehead against the cool of the mirror.

Well, it's nice to know I can take a punch at least. That I don't dissolve. That my atoms don't fly apart under pressure.

'Course, I don't fight back either . . . apparently.

Three more PBRs and a half a pack of Marlboro Reds later, Kat is still MIA, and I find myself sitting at the bar with a shot of tequila in my hands . . . again.

"It's on me." Suit Guy steps into my peripheral and takes a cocky seat next to me.

"It's alright, man." I keep my head forward but wave a dismissive hand his way.

"No, really. I'll get it. And it's not 'man,' it's Dave."

"Well, isn't that convenient?" I down my free shot and wince, sucking on a dried-up slice of lemon.

"Surprisingly, I've seen you."

"What? Pre-hardcore bitch fight?"

"Yeah. You used to sit in the Last Drop. Sometimes writing."

"Right."

"Haven't seen you lately, come to think of it."

"I've been busy."

He's incredibly laid back. Normally, I'd assume he was hitting on me, but with this guy, I'm not entirely sure. There isn't a nerve in sight.

"And you are?"

"What?"

"Your name. I'm Dave. And you are?" He extends his hand to me, keeping his elbow resting on the bar. Right, my name. Don't get asked that often.

Can't be fucked to think of anything interesting. Go with an old standby.

"Alice." I shake his hand.

"I don't want you to think I'm a crazy stalker or anything, but I think I saw you reading *Bright Lights, Big City* in there once, ages ago."

"Yeah, and . . . ?"

"Good one."

"Yeah, it is."

"A little before your time, I'd suppose."

"Don't have to be forty to be able to comprehend an eighties cocaine novel."

"Apparently not. And I'm thirty-eight."

"Oh right, sorry." I shrug in an I'm-not-really-sorry kind of way.

He downs the last of his beer and orders two more. I can't decide if I think this cheeky ordering of drinks without asking is sneaky or gentlemanly.

Not that I'm one to pass up a free drink, either way.

"Thanks." When the bartender sets the beers in front of us.

"No problem."

I go to light a cigarette and he's there with a lighter. A Zippo. Classic silver. No emblems.

Man, this guy is right out of one of those rare *good* movies. Something dark-funny. With an uplifting ending that somehow manages to not annoy the shit out of you.

Something with Robert Downey Jr. in it.

Wonder Boys.

"So what are you supposed to be? My knight in shining armor or something?"

"No. Why? You looking for one?"

"No."

Yes.

Daniel used to be like this sometimes. Most of the time when we first started dating. Slick. Cool. Like, movie cool. Five o'clock shadow, cigarette bobbing on his lip with his mumblings. That dark wool coat he had. With the big buttons. In the winter he looked like Lane Coutell. Waiting for Franny on the train platform, shielding his neck and cigarette with that stiff wool collar. Dad taught him to make the perfect martini and he was thrilled. Didn't drink anything else for months. He was New York, 1961. He was Wall Street, late-night jazz clubs, the Hamptons, kid gloves, Yale football games.

But only because he chose to be. He was forty years too late. His parents were forty grand a year too poor. His city was ninety-nine miles too far south.

He told me once, "Whenever I make a decision— what to say, how to act, about the kind of person I want to be, whether I smoke, what I drink—I just do whatever a really good character in a really good movie would do. Something with Gregory Peck in it."

I loved that. Love that. Present tense.

I adopted it immediately. I started drinking Jim Beam and ginger ale instead of watery lager. Smoking unfiltered cigarettes. Wearing huge plastic sunglasses. Before they were hip again.

Romantic Appeal. That indefinable something that so many things have, that just make them . . . well, not cooler . . . just classier . . .

Classic.

And this guy, he has the script down.

The lights in the bar flicker on, pinching my eyes.

Drinking-up time.

"Dammit. Isn't there anywhere decent to drink in this city after two?"

"Well." He smiles. "Not in *this* city."

Fuck. I'm going to Jersey again.

Driving down the Atlantic City Expressway my hair flickers in the breeze that wafts through the sunroof of his black Beamer.

What am I doing in a fucking Beamer, on the fucking expressway, with a fucking stranger, at two in the fucking morning? Who the fuck do I think I am? Kat?

Well, she seems a hell of a lot happier than me.

There's a Creedence album in the CD player. It's on "Lodi." God, call me a hick, I fucking love CCR.

"Hey." He doesn't take his eyes off the road.

"Yeah?"

"You wanna cut up a couple of lines?"

As if this guy *wouldn't* have coke.

"Yeah, sure."

"There's a Baggie in the glove compartment, and CD cases on the floor. I'm a bit of a slob."

Right.

"Alright, man. Just try and keep this thing steady."

"Don't you worry about that. And it's Dave."

"What?"

"Not 'man.' I'm Dave. You're Alice."

No I'm not. "Right. Sorry." This guy's trying to school me on manners.

Well, someone probably should.

Is this why I love My Stranger? Do I just want someone older? Someone who knows who he is, so he can tell me who to be?

Probably.

My Stranger. This is wrong. It's not happening the way it was supposed to. Why am I here and not on his doorstep?

Why am I still feeling so empty when he was supposed to fill me up?

Because of that woman. And what I did to her.

But tonight is tonight. Tonight I can't dive back into that. I'm weak, my strength zapped. My determination flagging.

And besides, this man's here. He's solid. Something real.

He's present.

Tonight, I'm Kat.

We top a crest in the road and there it is. Atlantic City sprawling in front of us. Neon comes in such ludicrous colors. Everything glares and blinks. Massive hotel casinos shoulder each other for space. Giant video billboards advertise Jimmy Buffett, Hanson, two-for-one lobster dinner deals. This city is running at a million watts, twenty-four hours a day. It's sapping the already dilapidated grid. Sucking every last drop of power this planet is dribbling.

What a waste. What an indescribable waste. What an unholy altar to the excess of American culture. The money. The power.

I suck up my line of coke.

If they were anything but drugs I'd be bored of them by now.

"What do you want me to do with this?" His line.

"Snort it. I'll have some when we park." I do. "So where to? Caesars? Harrah's? Borgata?"

"I wanna play roulette." I don't know why. There's something . . . appealing.

"Well, that doesn't narrow it down."

"You pick."

"Right. Caesars it is."

We pull up outside and he tosses his keys to the valet. Sliding a presumptuous arm around my waist, he leads me into the lobby without turning around to watch his car pull out safely.

On the floor he grabs a waitress. She's wearing what is basically a one-piece bathing suit and fishnet stocking. It's edged in sequins, and she doesn't quite have the body to be wearing this getup. I feel degraded for her.

"Um, Beam, on the rocks." Jim Beam again. "And you?"

"Just a beer. A Corona."

"Aw, come on. It's free."

"And a shot of tequila."

"We'll be by the roulette wheels." He tosses her a fiver to ensure that she'll actually come find us.

We wander through rows of blinking, clanging slot machines and video poker screens until we find the roulette tables.

"Here." He hands me a hundred-dollar bill. "Pick a number. But if you're gonna do it, do it right. Don't take the easy bet, black or red. Pick *one* number. No risk, no gain, right?"

No risk. No gain.

I don't think I've ever seen a hundred-dollar bill before. What is it they say? Ten percent of all hundred-dollar bills have traces of cocaine on them. Or is it the other way around. Ninety percent? I contemplate licking it for effect.

"I don't want this."

"You can split the winnings with me. Fifty-fifty. I consider it an investment. You look lucky."

Oh yeah. He's really got my number.

I slide the bill to the . . . what's he called? It's not cards so he can't be a dealer. He slides me back two black chips.

I put them on 2 without even really thinking about

it. But it makes sense to me. My birthday is 12/22/82, Mom's is 2/27, Dad's is the 25th. . . . Daniel's is 2/22. Everywhere twos.

You can find whatever you're looking for if you look hard enough.

The not-dealer closes the betting, lets the wheel spin, and drops the little white ball onto it. It clatters and clacks satisfyingly across the whirring numbers, settles into the outside gutter and spins there until the wheel begins to slow. Then it drops. Gravity deciding its fate and, in a small way, mine and that of the rest of the sad wanderers standing around this table with me.

The waitress saunters up behind us.

"Beam, Corona, and a shot of tequila."

I turn and down the tequila, slamming the shot glass back on her little black tray. She does not look amused.

And just as I lift my beer:

"Black two," the not-dealer states, and looks up at me from under his eyebrows, as if I cheated somehow.

He slides a stack of chips over to me.

"How much did I just win?" I whisper to Robert Downey, who is standing behind me.

"Thirty-five hundred. You gonna walk away and cash that out, or ride it?"

What am I, some kind of jackass?

•   •   •

At the Cash Out window I am entirely impressed and turned on by the stack of hundreds the teller has just handed me. I want to change them into ones, strip down naked, and roll around in them, *Indecent Proposal* style.

"Half of this is yours," I say, gesturing at Jr. with a fistful of Benjamins.

"OK. I'll take seventeen. You take eighteen. It's easier."

I have eighteen hundred dollars. How did that just happen?

"Well, now we can afford to blow a bunch of money on video poker. I told you you were lucky."

As we sit at the video poker machines, sliding in dollar after dollar, he starts talking about his job. I'm not listening. I'm completely glazed over. Watching the card graphics turn over. The waitress keeps the Coronas and tequilas coming, and soon I go from glazed to blurred. I'm heavy-handedly slapping the big plastic buttons, having no idea if I'm up or down. Not caring.

He's rambling, and I hate him. I'm not charmed, I'm not fooled, I'm just here. Which law of motion is that? A stationary object will remain stationary until a force is acted upon it . . . or something like that. That's me. The stationary object. I'm sick of trying to be the force, because apparently the object doesn't necessarily move in the direction you want it to. From now on I'm passive. I'll let life act upon me. All my actions will be reactions.

I give up.

I can't make out what's on the screen anymore, and as usual, I've lost track of my tequila intake. I'm having trouble even staying on the high stool in front of the machine, although I'm not sure how it's possible to get so drunk you can't even sit.

As I waver and catch myself for the umpteenth time, I feel an arm slide around my waist and a hand grasp my elbow.

Oh right, Robert Downey . . . I almost forgot he was here. Sly bastard.

"I'm pretty wasted, too. Maybe we should get a room."

I don't even bother trying to respond but allow him to guide me off my stool and through the floor to the lobby. Passive. That's me. An object being acted upon.

At the front desk he releases me and I slump over, my head on my arms, my arms on the desk. I hear murmured talking but don't even bother trying to make out the words.

In the elevator, I lean against him, for support more

than anything else. He has his hand up my shirt and under my bra, thumbing my nipple.

When he unlocks the door to our room, I stumble in and collapse on the bed. Curl up. Fetal. He pulls on my hip so that I roll onto my back. My head flops to one side and I shut my eyes. The room is spinning, and I can just about feel him undoing the zip on my jeans and pulling them off. I start to make a pathetic grasp at holding them on.

"Hey, fuck off," I slur.

"Yeah, right. Look at you. What the fuck are you gonna do about it?"

He's right. Why bother?

My jeans come off and my underwear with them. I hear his zip going as well. I don't bother opening my eyes. I know what I'd see. Him leering, cocky smile gone, replaced with a sneer, cock out, half hard, standing over me.

He rolls me over on my stomach. Pulls me by the hips, so I'm on my knees, with my face pressed into the pillow. I feel slight pressure as he pushes himself into me with a low groan. I'm pretty sure he didn't take the time to put on a condom. I half wish I had the clap or something.

He forces me back and forth on his cock, and my face slides back and forth across the pillow with the movement.

"Move your fucking ass, bitch."

But I don't.

He pounds away and doesn't seem to notice.

"God, you're a dumb fucking slut." He spits at my back. He's right. I raise a hand behind me and give him the finger. Then his hand is in my hair. Gripping hard, he gives it a sharp yank. "I'm gonna fucking cum inside you."

Wonderful.

He slams into me harder and harder, grunting like a fucking farm animal.

"Well, then get it the fuck over with," I try to say, but it just comes out as muffled gibberish. Plus, he's not even listening.

Finally he digs his fingers into my hips, pushes himself deep inside me, and shudders.

Without missing a beat he pulls out and wipes his dick on my ass.

An object to be acted upon.

I wake up to light tearing at my eyes and piercing the back of my brain. My head feels like it's been kicked in. To be fair, so does the rest of me. The light is coming from a slit in the heavy hotel curtains.

The spot next to me in the bed is empty. The sheets reassuringly cool. The room quiet. Like maybe it didn't really happen. A nightmare.

I sit up and look around. There's no sign of him. Not a jacket or a shoe.

I think about the eighteen hundred, and I feel like a prostitute.

I move to get out of the bed and notice that the sheets are wet.

I'm bleeding. But not from him. I don't know how I know, I just do.

The dry, sticky pull of my own menstrual blood and his leaking cum between my thighs makes me realize, and not for the first time, that it doesn't take much to make new people. Just sticky, dripping fluids.

Can I change my DNA?

Make my genes more than they are just by sheer force of will? Make my eggs somehow more worthy of My Stranger's sperm?

One gooey incongruous mess that eventually divides into something complete and beautiful.

I cautiously rise in the bed and put both feet on the floor. I'm trembling slightly.

Why do I keep doing this shit to myself? Why do I feel the need to unravel myself, stitch by stitch?

They say that sometimes you have to hit rock bottom before anything gets better. But what if, once you hit rock bottom, you just scratch and claw and dig yourself down in the dark and find a cave where you can curl up and die?

There's blood and cum smeared on my inner thighs,

and my body feels sore. Battered. So I take advantage of the shower.

I stand under the stream for what feels like forever. Breathing slowly and deeply. Desperate to regain my composure. To steady myself. But it doesn't quite happen.

I dry myself and get dressed, stuffing a wad of toilet paper in my underwear for lack of a tampon. I scan the room for my bag. It's by the door, all its contents strewn on the floor around it. At first I assume this is because I dropped it on the way in, but when I look in my wallet, it's all gone. The cash anyway. At least he was gentleman enough to leave the plastic.

I chuck the wallet heavily against the far wall.

Fucking idiot. Dumb fucking drunk slut idiot.

The man at the front desk looks at me funny as he directs me to the bus station. I wonder what his eyeballs would feel like if I jammed my fingers into them.

It's bizarrely bright and sunny for the end of September, and I feel as though the weather is mocking me. "I don't give a shit if you're having a crappy time of it, I'm going to give everyone else a beautiful day." Bastard fucking sky.

I pass fat tourists in ugly shirts and sun hats, sunglasses attached to neon-colored nylon that loops behind their sunburned ears. Hauling their fat, screaming children through the dry, stifling AC streets. Off-seasoners. Too poor to stay here in the summer. Banking on global warming to give them beach weather in the autumn.

I have to get out of Jersey.

The next bus to Philly isn't for an hour so I curl up on a bench, head propped on my balled-up hoodie, eyes closed.

I think about Lazy Line Painter Jane, sleeping at bus stops, wondering how she got her name.

That really is a good song.

I feel as though I should be getting flashes. Of that horrible man smirking at me. Of the print on that pillowcase. Like I should be feeling nauseous and violated.

But I don't. I don't feel anything.

Sex is meaningless.

The first time Daniel and I had sex wasn't meaningless. The first night we met I came on to him. But he was having none of it. He stayed in my bed. Slept next to me, kissed me. But he wouldn't fuck me. Even stopped me from trying to go down on him. I was almost offended. It wasn't until a few weeks later, at one of our then common sleepovers, that I turned to him and said, "So are you ever gonna sleep with me?"

"But I do sleep with you. Almost every night this week."

"Very funny, you know what I mean."

"Yes. I just hate that phrase."

"What do you say?"

"Fucking."

"No you don't."

"OK, how about 'making time'?"

"Ha. I like that one. How very Holden of you."

"Fair enough. But, yes. I mean, I'd like to. I just didn't want to make a promise I couldn't keep."

I didn't want any promises. I wanted to get fucked. And I told him.

"I don't want any promises, I just want to get fucked."

He laughed, and then we fucked.

And the sex was good. It wasn't mind-blowing. I didn't cum. But that didn't matter. It wasn't sex for the sake of sex, it was . . . getting next to someone. It had a purpose. I wanted to know him. Get inside him.

I sleep most of the way back to Philly. Nodding in and out of dreams about caged animals and people I've never met.

When I get off the bus in the middle of Chinatown, I automatically head toward my place.

But I realize rather quickly that that is not where I want to be. I can't face the idea of holing myself back up in that suffocating room. Smoking a joint, listening to Echo & the Bunnymen, and succumbing to my worthlessness.

But where can I go?

I could hop a train back up to Jay's. But New York is fucking expensive, and I'm already running on credit. Besides, there'd be too many questions to try to avoid.

Could always go hang out with the stoners at Chipmunk's, but I'd probably end up strangling one of them.

Mom's?

More questions. And how could I look at her really? When did I become such a disappointment? There was a time when I was promising . . . gifted even. People expected things from me. And here I am . . . losing it.

It's probably already lost.

I briefly consider calling Dad and asking him to fly me out. To take some time out of the city, out of the state, where there wouldn't be any questions. Dad wouldn't even know there were questions to be asked.

But no, running away only prolongs things, and besides, I'd never keep up a convincing exterior long enough.

No, not Dad's. I feel lost, so I need to go some-where I can feel found.

I know there's only one place I really want to be.

Outside the door I raise my knuckles to knock but stop short. I rest my head on the door frame and take a deep breath.

Just do this. It's gonna be alright. He won't throw you out. Hopefully.

I knock.

After a few seconds I hear the chain rattle. The door opens to Daniel, already scowling, having, I assume, spied me through the peephole before he answered.

"What're you doing here?" Inside, the threshold where he's standing is raised a step from where I stand on the mat outside. He's already a head taller than I am, and this makes him loom over me.

"I'm not sure. I just . . . I needed to go somewhere."

"Well, you're here now. Might as well come in."

"Right." I pull my arms in close to me and step up into the house, following him through the hall to the kitchen.

I really don't know why I'm here. Why not? Even amid the awkwardness, I suddenly feel very comfort-able.

In the kitchen I pull a stool up to the counter sepa-rating it from the living room.

"I'm not interrupting anything, am I? Do you have plans right now?"

"If you really cared, you wouldn't have just shown up." He leans against the counter across the room from me. Keeping his distance.

"Fair enough."

"You still say that all the time, or you just regressing around me?"

"What?"

"That whole 'fair enough' thing. That's my line."

"Right. Guess it just stuck."

"So why are you here? Really. To be honest, I didn't think we left things at the 'Hey, drop round anytime' stage." His hair has been cut shorter than usual. It makes him look younger.

"No. We didn't. And I'm sorry. But like I said, I just really needed somewhere to go. This just . . . I don't know. Made sense at the time."

"And does it still now?"

"Dunno. Yeah, in a way."

"Right."

I want to tell him. Tell him that I'm losing it. That I don't know where I am or what I'm doing. Who I'm meant to be. I want to tell him all the shit I've managed to get myself into. How I just want someone to make it all go away. But I look at him and can't. Can't heap that on him after all the heaping I've done.

"I'll go if you want, but I'd really appreciate it if I

could just hang out here for a bit." I can see him soften a little, and I'm honestly grateful.

"Yeah. Fine. But what the fuck did you do to your face?" He opens the fridge and pulls out two bottles of lager. He opens a drawer and removes a bottle opener. Pops the caps. It's one of those old-fashioned openers. All metal. A church key.

"Ha. Bar fight. What else?"

He hands a bottle to me and swigs out of the other.

"Thanks."

He pulls up the second stool and straddles it in front of me.

"You alright?"

"No." I laugh a little, but then it comes to me. What I let that horrible man do to me. What I did to that woman. The fight, the cat, Frat Boy. The hate. The anger. The last two weeks. The last six months. The last sixteen years? How long has this been going on? When did this all start?

And I sob. Just sob into my hands, and then Daniel draws me in with his arms, into his chest.

And he doesn't rub my back or stroke my hair. He doesn't ask me why. He just holds me there and lets me cry.

The first night I met Daniel I knew. I saw him when he came in the door, and I just knew he was someone.

That someday he'd be an important memory, a feature in all my stories. A way of marking time in my history. Before Daniel and after. BD and AD.

Our housewarming party sophomore year. I'd just moved into that house in Northern Liberties with Paul and Adam. Daniel was an old friend of Paul's. Hadn't seen each other in years. But for some reason, that day they ran into each other on campus, and Paul invited him to our party. And for some reason he came, and when he walked in the door, for some reason, I knew. We smoked all those cigarettes in the backyard, huddled under the awning to keep out of the rain. And by the end of the night, when everyone had started to trail off . . . I was drunk, straddling him on the sofa in the living room. Giggling, flirting. When I knew how to flirt. I had my hair up in one of those too-high ponytails, and a single stray strand hung in front of my face, dusting his sandy, stubbled chin. He held his glowing cigarette up to the end of the solitary, floating hair, and it sizzled and cracked, curling in on itself, blackening and becoming ash. He said sorry, that he didn't know why he had done that. I said I didn't mind. . . . I didn't.

That it was sexy . . . it was.

We stayed up all night. I didn't have a bed then, just a mattress on the floor. He kept me up, recounting the plots of Gordon Korman books he had read as a kid. Making up stories, making me laugh. My face and stomach muscles ached for days from laughing so hard.

He told me later how much he had enjoyed that first night; how making me laugh made him feel real. How his being able to make me laugh like that was why he fell for me. How he knew also, right from the beginning, right from when he walked in the door.

And the fact that he wouldn't fuck me that night . . .

That was probably why I fell for him.

The next day, after the party, Paul and I drove him home in Paul's pickup truck. We pulled up outside his dorm at Temple, and he said, "Wait a minute. I have something for you."

And he went inside and got me his copy of one of the books he'd told me about the night before. *Don't Care High*. And I read it that night and underlined this great line I found. "Sometimes ordinary things can be glorious." It really struck me at the time. I really believed that. Adopted it as my personal creed.

God, I was only nineteen.

We could have been. We could have been something good.

And for a moment I want to break his embrace. Hold his face in my hands and kiss him. Tell him that I'm sorry. That we could still do it. That we could try again.

But I don't have to because he does it.

He puts his hands on my shoulders and pushes me

away from his body, lifts my chin, and looks in my eyes.

"Why did you really come here?"

I had nowhere else to go.

But I don't answer. Just look back. He tips my chin farther and leans in, kisses me gently, letting his bottom lip rest between both of mine. I don't kiss back, but I don't pull away, either.

"What was that for?"

"I don't know. It just made sense at the time." He's in his own movie now. Scripting perfect lines as he goes. He wants me to respond with "And does it still now?" But I don't.

"I thought you hated me."

"I do."

Then he leans in again. Kisses me again, this time parting his lips slightly, and mine part with them.

I'm kissing him back and there's a hand on my waist. I reach up and tug on his earlobe in that way that I always used to, and haven't done with anyone since.

And it all feels so familiar. Like a rerun of an old TV show. Like one of those episodes of *Cheers* you've seen a hundred times but watch again because you know it so well and it's comforting.

And I know that I could go to bed with him tonight. And that it would be good, and sweet, and I would probably cry, but not in a bad way. And we could start this again from the beginning. Rewind the tape.

But that's just it. We'd be starting the same tape over, and the ending would always be the same.

I can't go back. This could never be new again. We've been here before.

People say life is cyclical. A circle repeating itself. A snake swallowing its tail. But it's not cyclical really. It's linear. A straight line. Leaving old things behind and coming across new ones along the way. It carries on in one direction forever. If you go back you'll just be treading old ground.

I pull away and look down.

I know that what I'm really here for isn't sex, it's confession. I must confess my sins if I want to be born again. That's how it works, right?

"Daniel, I killed the cat."

"What do you mean?" He sits up.

I'm afraid of losing my composure again and can feel thick, hard sobs rising in my throat. I swallow them.

"I left him. I left Sal, for a week. He died. I let him die."

"You left him? You fucking forgot about him?" His cheeks go flush and his eyelids flood. "What the fuck's the matter with you?"

"I know. I'm selfish and horrible . . . and I don't want to be that anymore. So I have to go now."

"Fucking right you have to go. You sick fuck." He's on his feet, fists clenched, trying unsuccessfully to hold back tears.

I hesitate. Feel I should say something else. Anything.

"Daniel, I'm sorry." And I am. I really, really am.

"Now. Get out now."

I collect my things and make my way to the front
door. He stays in the kitchen, back to me, as I open the
door and step out into the peach and purple night.

I stand on his stoop for a moment and allow myself
to cry for a bit. For Sal, for me and Daniel. For things
that could have been but never will be. For the long,
straight road ahead that can only be traveled in one
direction.

For My Stranger. How, unknowingly, he brought
me to this moment. Brought me through the dark.

And for how he wouldn't notice if I disappeared
today.

I saw a man on a train, reading a book that reminded
me of Daniel. And without ever knowing I exist, that
man changed me.

Sometimes ordinary things can be glorious.

I still believe that.